Enemies and Other Strangers

ENEMIES AND OTHER STRANGERS

stories
by

CHRISTOPHER LEACH

J M DENT AND SONS LTD
London   Melbourne

First published 1986
© Christopher Leach 1986

This book is set in 10½ on 12½ Linotron 202 Sabon by
Inforum Ltd, Portsmouth
Printed in Great Britain by
Biddles Ltd, Guildford for
J.M. Dent & Sons Ltd
Aldine House, 33 Welbeck Street, London W1M 8LX

British Library Cataloguing in Publication Data

Leach, Christopher, *1925*–
    Enemies and other strangers: short stories.
    I. Title
    823'.914[F]   PR6062.E18

ISBN 0–460–04686–1

Contents

To
BOB JEFFERY

STRANGERS

As a consequence, he was late for the train. It was as he feared: every compartment full, the same pig faces staring back at him, the tables already awash with paper cups. Soon there would be spilt coffee, crumbs, crushed sandwich-plastic, drunks, the same pig faces asleep, open mouths, teeth . . .

He had walked almost the length of the train, and was now approaching the engine. It throbbed. The driver was talking to a porter. Sunlight cut the engine in two. All around was the roar of the station, people saying goodbye.

He couldn't believe his luck. It was completely, beautifully empty. The long walk had been worth it. *And* a non-smoker.

He smiled, and opened the door. And it was clean: a bonus. He took off his dark overcoat, folded it carefully, and put it on a seat. He put his hat and briefcase on another; and on the others he put his scarf, his gloves, and his folded *Times* and *Telegraph*. The compartment secured, he closed the door.

Humming to himself, he looked in the mirror, examined his teeth, pressed his hair in place with the flat of his hands – and sat in the window-seat, facing the engine, the distance.

He looked at his right hand resting on the ledge. It was a good hand: clean, with carefully-tended nails. He was proud of it.

His eyes lifted to the tracks. The contrast: metal and rust, grease, grass struggling to live. Empty cigarette-packs. The smear of industry.

*

The door opened. A man stood there, almost a replica of himself: dark coat, hat, gloves, briefcase. A man who began to push his way in, grunting.

'I'm sorry,' said Baxter, motioning to his own coat, hat, briefcase, papers: 'they're taken.'

I

'Taken?' said the man: 'all of them?'

''Fraid so,' said Baxter. 'They've gone to the bar. Sorry.'

The man looked at him, opened his mouth to say something . . .

'It's not a position I like to find myself in,' said Baxter. 'It makes me appear . . . inconsiderate. Move something, if you like.'

'No, I'll try further on,' said the man, and closed the door.

Baxter sat back. Above the metal and the grease the sky was untouched.

'Come on,' he said: 'get moving.'

As if in answer, arranged, a whistle sounded; and was echoed, fainter. The train jerked and took the strain. On the platform a man and a woman began waving. Smoothly sunlight invaded the compartment, warmed Baxter's cheek.

He waited five minutes; then cleared the seats, putting everything but the papers in the rack above his head.

He sat down again and rested his head against the warm fabric of the seat. He would close his eyes until the train cleared the city: until fields and woods took over: the natural world.

The train sped on. Bars of shadow crossed his eyelids . . .

*

He heard the door open. The ticket-collector. He opened his eyes. But it was not.

Two children stood in the doorway, behind them a woman. The children's eyes were large and apprehensive. Their hands clutched games and books. Behind the woman the city was still there: high-rise blocks catching the last of the afternoon sun.

'I'm sorry,' said the woman: 'the train's packed.'

Baxter looked away from them, pressed himself into the hardness of wood and metal.

'Do you mind?' said the woman.

Baxter said nothing.

'In you go,' said the woman, quietly. 'You go there, Philip. And you next to me, Anne.'

He heard the rustle of their movements, felt his section of seating shift as the boy wriggled himself comfortable. The door closed.

The woman's voice was a whisper.

2

'Now, what are you going to do, Anne?'

'Read my book,' said the girl, softly.

'And you, Philip?'

'Thought I'd try my game.'

'Is it noisy?'

'It's only cards.'

'All right. But, *quietly*.'

'What are *you* going to do, Mummy?' said the girl.

'I may sleep,' she said. 'I feel very tired. I may do the crossword. Quiet now: no more questions.'

There was silence.

Baxter watched a sign grow by the side of the tracks: *Come Home to A Coal Fire this Winter*. The dream family warmed themselves in the dream living-room, complete with cat. The flames coloured the room an angry red. Gone. But the anger remained, imprinted on a lonely autumnal park.

Now the city fell back. Detached houses, safe in their isolation, lived in the centre of large gardens. There were empty tennis-courts, the cold wink of a swimming-pool. Behind the trees on the horizon the orange sun winked back. A man was working in an allotment, digging at something.

*

The children were exceptionally quiet. Turn of a page, the lisp of card. Baxter looked at them.

The boy kept his head down, playing a game that needed two; but the girl shot Baxter a quick, half-smiling, nervous glance. His face did not change, and she returned to her book. She held it very tightly, her fingers hiding the title. He could only read *The Amazing*.

He moved from her to the woman. Head back, eyes and mouth closed, she was not asleep.

He settled himself in his corner, folded his arms in the last of the angled sun, and began with her hair.

It was a kind of brown: neither one thing nor the other. Nothing definite. *Mousy*? It was thick and had no style. Some might call it free, but he would say untidy. It framed a pale face, long and narrow, with surprisingly full lips. A long brown coat with large yellow-bone buttons was open to show a plain yellow sweater and a green plaid skirt. Her hands were crossed in her lap, and her brogues crossed at her ankles: an elongated symmetry. He thought of her body: small-breasted, long-thighed . . . He found she was staring directly at him, and turned his head to the window, the racing poplars.

When he glanced back, she closed her eyes again.

He considered the girl. She was slightly older than the boy. She was not reading. Holding the book in hard hands, her eyes were unmoving. Her fine fair hair was tied with a blue ribbon. Her eyelashes were golden, and she had her mother's full lips. A blue anorak matched the ribbon . . . Once again he found himself stared at.

The girl said: 'Would you like a sweet?'

Her voice was an invisible wire that tugged at everyone. The woman opened her eyes and sat up.

'Anne, what did we agree?'

'I only . . .'

'You've spoiled it now,' said the boy. He looked swiftly at Baxter, and away.

'I only . . .' said the girl again.

'Do you *want* a sweet?' said the woman to Baxter.

'No.'

'He doesn't want a sweet,' said the woman.

'I'll have one,' said the boy.

The woman sighed.

'*Now* who's spoiling it?' she said.

'She started it . . .'

'Give him one, Anne.'

The girl put her book to one side. It was *The Amazing Zoo*. She took a paper bag from her anorak.

'Do you want one, Mummy?'

'No. Hurry up, please.'

Even against the rush and creak of the train, the unwrapping of the sweets was loud, causing the woman to shake her head. She sat back and closed her eyes again. The girl picked up her book, the boy shuffled his cards.

*

The boy had black hair. Head down, the nape of his neck was very white and clean. The small pressures of the spine. He wore a green anorak and short grey trousers. His legs were stick-like, like a bird's; his knees marked with old scars. His nails were bitten and his fingers looked sore. When Baxter looked away, the cards began moving again.

A uniform appeared behind the glass, and the door slid back.

'Tickets, please.'

The girl relaxed.

The collector steadied himself against the doorframe. He took the tickets from the woman.

'These are second-class, madam.'

'Yes, I'm sorry: there was no room . . .'

'There *are* some seats, back there. I'll have to ask you to move. Or pay the extra . . .'

'I'll pay the extra. How much is it?'

'I'll have to work it out. We'll forget about the kids.' He took out a pad. He was an elderly man in a uniform too small for his bulk: the blue cloth strained. He looked over his spectacles at the children. 'Soon be Christmas, eh?'

'Yes,' they said together. They gave short, forced laughs, and looked at Baxter.

He turned to the window. The sun had gone now, and the clouds of night were massing overhead: a dramatic piling of blues and blacks, edged with fire.

'One pound, seventy-five, madam.' As she searched for the correct money, he said: 'And *yours*, sir?'

Baxter opened his wallet and showed his first-class season-ticket.

'Thank you very much, sir.'

The collector took the money, tore a page from the pad and gave it to the woman.

'Thank you, madam,' he said, and prepared to leave.

'Would you like a sweet?' said the girl.

Half his body in the corridor, he said: 'I wouldn't say no. What are they?'

'Toffee whirls,' said the girl, and held out the bag.

'My favourite,' he said. He took one. 'This'll keep me going till Portsmouth. Thanks, love.'

The door closed.

*

The boy shuffled the cards again. The girl hummed softly, swinging her legs back and forth, the book closed in her hands. The woman was doing the *Mail* crossword.

Lights were appearing in houses by the track. He glimpsed honey-coloured interiors: a woman at a sink; a man outlined at a back door, waiting for a dog. Headlamps topped a rise, dipped.

The girl's eyes met his, and once more she gave him that nervous half-smile with closed lips. And once again he did not respond, and she looked away.

He thought of children's untidy bedrooms: of one-eyed dolls and scattered pieces of model aeroplane. He went out of their rooms and walked the rest of the house: the unmade marriage-bed, the dressing-table with hairs in the comb; the bathroom with the uncapped toothpaste, the laundry-basket full of damp towels; the kitchen with its empty cereal-packs and saucers of dried cat-food; the stacked magazines in the living-room, socks drying by the fire; and, outside, in the darkening garden, the leaf-littered pool where no goldfish thrived.

The train began to slow, and Baxter recognised the landmarks: the lit greenhouses of Humbold's Nursery; the spire of the church, the golden window of the estate-agent's; the start of the High Street. He stood up and reached to the rack.

The woman glanced out into the corridor. A man passed, anxious to be home. She put her pen away and folded the paper into her bag.

'Ready, Philip?' she said.

'Yes,' he said. He tapped the cards into shape, and fitted them into the box. The girl slid off her seat and gave the book and her unused game to her mother. The woman stood up and began to button her coat.

'Can we wait in the corridor?' said the boy.

'Yes,' she said.

They went out, stood together grasping the rail, and stared through their reflections at the moving platform.

Scarf and coat in place, Baxter pulled on his gloves. They felt strangely cold, as though someone older had worn them. The train stopped with a jolt, and the woman swayed. He put out a hand, but did not touch her. Picking up his briefcase, he followed her out.

The man who was anxious to be home opened the door, left it wide, and hurried to the barrier.

'Let me go first, Anne,' said the woman. She helped the children down.

The air still held a touch of the day's unexpected sun, but behind the leafless trees at the end of the forecourt, winter waited.

*

He followed them to the car-park. He unlocked the car, and the children got in the back. He waited for the woman to go around to her seat, but she shut the door on the children, and faced him.

'Have you made up your mind?' she said.

'No,' he said.

Her free hair stirred.

'Well, I *have*,' she said, and her words and her face were stone.

*

She went around the front of the car and got in. He sat behind the wheel and put the key into the ignition.

Something touched his shoulder. It was the girl's hand.

'Is it all right for us to talk to you *now*, Daddy?' she said.

The Smallest Man In The World

For private reasons I had to get away. I took a pin, closed my eyes, and stuck it in a map. The name was Sheldon. I looked it up in the Automobile Association Handbook, and chose the Heathview Hotel, thinking of a wide and lonely mixture of sheep-cropped grass and gorse. *You're lucky* said the girl, when I phoned: *you've got the last single.*

Sheldon sat in flat Cheshire country. Approaching it, I saw signs nailed to trees: *May Day Fair*, and cursed my luck – I wanted rest and sleep, not a gathering of drunken yokels and lustful teenagers. But I had committed myself, and believed in the precise ordering of fate.

The hotel was small and comfortable. My room faced the fairground: so much for lonely expanses. *You're lucky, sir* said the old man, standing with me at the window: *people'd give a lot for this view.*

Fragile towers soared, holding planes and perilous seats and space-craft. Generators hummed. Alsatians, tethered to luxurious trailers, lay panting in long grass. Organs were playing: abrupt skirls of space-age music.

I went down to lunch.

*

The food was good, and the wine made me sleepy. That, and the pressures of the past weeks, took me back to my room. I lay on the bedcovers, and slept deeply for most of the afternoon. I awoke refreshed, and went to the window. People swarmed in the fairground, and the towers were a metal forest, busy with multi-coloured lights. I took a shower, and went downstairs.

'You missed the procession,' said the girl at the desk.

I went out.

The air was made of diesel-fumes, fried onions and trodden

9

grass. I walked around the fenced perimeter. There was a tawdriness that had escaped me in childhood: battered sideshows, scraped paintwork, dulled gilt; the weatherbeaten stare of monsters and mermaids.

The town was divided. Huge men marked with grease and tattoos drank from beer-cans in streets made for gentility. There was a foreignness abroad, and the locals were shaken and exhilarated by difference.

In an hour I had seen all I wanted: it was just another English town in the rut of an old tradition. Flags were everywhere, and balloons bobbed above excited children, for whom everything was new.

I struck out for the surrounding country, and was soon alone with young wheat and barley, the trim lines of well-kept farms, the cries of peewits, the green scum of ponds. I sat on stiles and fences, but even with silence and unconcerned nature, peace would not come.

The day was dying in red as I turned back.

*

With the coming of dusk came magic. The fair was a circle of fire, warming the heavens and burning in the windows of houses. Travel-dirt was transformed by blue shadow, and the space between sideshows was soft like fur, touchable. Grass turned green, then red. Breaths of hamburger and hot-dog; screams aloft as lighted ovals dipped; girls with dolls whose new flesh squeaked; boys slamming punchballs for sex, ringing all the bells.

There was a Mouse-Circus, a Ghost Train, a House of Horror and a Journey to Mars.

I went into the Mouse-Circus. In a large tray covered with mesh, a hundred white mice climbed ladders, raced nowhere on spinning wheels, rode a railway, fell from wires, hurried through tunnels. Each was indistinguishable from the rest: same short white fur, same protuberant pink eyes, same twitching nose. Outside, the owner yawned, lit another cigarette.

A little way along, over increasingly flattened grass, was a green tent framed with winking lights. There was a sign: *The Four Marvels*. A woman in a beaded dress waved thick bare arms and a loop of tickets.

'Come on now, my lovelies! You won't believe your eyes! What about you, sir?'

I stepped back into the throng and read the bright notices: *See the Two-Headed Goat; The Bearded Lady; The Giant Sea-Monster; The Smallest Man In The World. 50p. Children Half-Price.*

'Thank you, lovey,' she said. She dropped the coin into a box and gave me a ticket. 'Now, come along, you people! It's an education, it is!'

Entering the tent, I found a sudden, almost cathedral-like quiet. Four separate booths had been set up, shielded from each other, and the crowd moved slowly from one to another.

In the first was the Two-Headed Goat. It stood in clean straw before a badly-painted backdrop of fields and hills. On one of the hills was a notice: *His name is Leslie. Do not feed.* There was a faint, sweet animal smell. The two heads, springing elegantly from the body, were perfect. They seemed to have separate existences: one was nuzzling a child who was stroking between its horns; the other looked away, chewing.

'Hallo, Leslie,' said the child.

In the second sat the Bearded Lady. The backdrop, by the same amateur artist, showed a country kitchen, hung with too many copper pans. She sat in a large floral armchair, and knitted. Like the goat, she seemed content, imperturbable. She said nothing, but smiled often, nodding regally. We stared at her thick brown moustache and wavy beard. And moved on.

In the next, the artist had painted the sea. Giant waves were fixed, motionless. Resting on a metal stand was a thick-walled glass tank. Inside the tank something moved: blue-black among restless weeds. Water bubbled in thin pipes, a moist heat. The thing came close, declared itself: half its body shredded.

'Don't call that a monster,' said a boy. 'It's only an octopus.'

The octopus reached the limit of its ocean, and turned back.

The last booth had a kind of magnificence. A different artist had been employed. The setting was a library. The fact that all the books were fake – long rows of empty spines – did not matter. The golden titles glowed, covering all three sides. Below them was a miniature table on which a lamp with an amber shade cast a warm circle over a decanter and an empty glass, leaving the rest of the booth in an intimate half-glow: as though we spied on some private pleasure. To the right of the table stood an expensive hi-fi system, two tall speakers, and a rack of records. Between the table and the hi-fi, the Smallest Man In The World sat reading in a miniature leather chair.

Whether he held the world record, I did not know. But he *was* the smallest man I had ever seen. Even the chair appeared a little too large: was he shrinking, even as we watched?

The book he read was made for a giant. He turned a page, seemingly oblivious of us, the intruders.

It was difficult to tell his age. His hair was black and plentiful, his round face unmarked. He wore a deep red, quilted smoking-jacket over a white shirt and a black cravat, his legs in black trousers with thin red piping. His feet, in shining black shoes, were inches off the eastern rug, whose yellow fringes ended in dark grassblades.

He turned another page.

The tent still held that cathedral-quiet. Outside, the fair roared on, laced with screams.

I was pushed to one side.

'Is that all you *do*?' said a voice.

*

The drunk rested a heavy hand on my shoulder. He was young, out for a good time with his mates, and he thrust his wet-lipped face forward. He waved his other hand in an arc.

'I said: is that all you bloody *do*?'

The smallest man looked up from the book, his round face rounder in the lamplight.

'Are you talking to me?' he said, and the words were shaped and spaced in deliberate contrast.

The drunk took his hand off my shoulder, and pressed against the rope that barred the way to the library.

'I bloody *am*!' he said. 'Fifty p to see a goat, some old dear knitting, a half-dead octopus, and now you just sitting there! We can all bloody read!'

'You surprise me,' said the smallest man, in the same calm, well-modulated voice: 'I would have guessed you'd never read a book in your life.'

Behind me a woman laughed.

The rope grew taut against the drunk's body.

'Very funny,' he said. 'What is it? – *Tom Thumb*?'

Now one of his mates laughed.

The smallest man inched back in his chair. He turned the spine of the book to face the drunk.

'It's Cicero,' he said. 'I'm sure you're familiar with him.'

'Never go to bed without him,' said the drunk. 'I'm not paying fifty p to watch you read. So, do something.'

The smallest man took a bookmark from the centre pages, marked his place, and put the book on the table. He shifted his body around, his small white hands grasped the decanter, and he half-filled the glass. He sat back again.

'Cheers,' he said, and drank. He took the glass from his lips. 'I'd offer you some, my friend, but I imagine you're a best-bitter man, yes?'

'Is that all you do, then?' said the drunk. 'That how you make your bread?: sitting there reading and drinking?'

The smallest man took another drink: I could smell whisky. By now the crowd in the tent, tired of the silent meekness of the goat, the smiling bearded lady, and the slow coldness of the octopus, thickened behind me: seeing in this confrontation a chance to become anonymous, to laugh as one.

'What do you suggest I do?' said the smallest man. 'Shall I read you some Cicero? Virgil, Homer? Or perhaps you prefer the moderns?: how about some Wallace Stevens?' He finished the whisky and linked those tiny fingers. 'Shall I speak Hamlet? Shall I dance, stand on my head, tell a few jokes? Did you hear the one about the ignorant drunk and the princeling?'

A voice called from the crowd.

'Let's hear one of your records!'

'I bet he's a heavy-metal freak!' shouted another.

At the word *freak*, the smallest man stiffened. His face grew hard, and his voice changed: even more controlled, distant.

'Very well,' he said: 'some music . . .'

He got off the chair and swung his body towards the hi-fi. At once, a kind of dignity vanished. On his feet, he was dwarf, midget, court-jester, pantomime clown, circus stooge. The crowd laughed, as one.

He got a painted stool, climbed on to it, and ran his fingers through the rack. He chose a record and took it carefully from its sleeve. He put it on the turntable.

'Quiet, please,' he said, and there was an authority that silenced us all.

The piano began, loud in the speakers, until he adjusted the volume. Still standing on the stool, swaying slightly, he clasped his hands in front of himself.

'A pound to anyone who knows the composer,' he said. His eyes, still below our level, moved over our faces. 'I'm sure my money's safe.'

'Erik Satie,' I heard myself say.

*

I had no desire for the money: it was an instinctive response, a sharing.

'Is he right?' said the drunk.

The smallest man, hands still clasped, nodded.

'He's right.'

'Well, where's the pound?'

'No, don't worry about that,' I said.

'Pay the man,' said the drunk.

The slow, measured dance continued as the smallest man got off the stool, crossed the rug, and stood near the rope. He looked up. His face was perfectly smooth, yet age was there, dusted with light make-up. His eyes, overbright, spoke of a day's drinking.

'What's a cultured man doing with this rabble?' he said.

'You paying him?' said the drunk.

'No, that's all right,' I said.

But a small hand was already inside the quilted jacket, and a pound appeared.

'Cheap at the price,' said the smallest man.

I shook my head.

'Take it,' he said.

The drunk took it and gave it to me.

'Thank you,' I said.

The drunk reached over the rope and rested his hand on the smallest man's head.

'How's your sex-life, short-arse?' he said. 'You getting any?'

14

There was a shifting behind me, and the crowd parted. The bearded lady, heavy with perfume, pushed through.

'Everything all right, Ralph?' she said.

The smallest man had moved out from under the drunk's hand, and was smoothing his hair. Behind him the music played on: stately, processional.

'Everything's fine, Virginia,' he said. 'Please don't interfere.'

The bearded lady looked at the drunk.

'Hallo, beautiful,' he said.

'You want to know about my sex-life, too?' she said.

He glanced at his mates, and back to her.

'I wouldn't mind, Virginia,' he said.

She seized him by the shoulders, and kneed him viciously in the crotch.

'That's yours finished for a while,' she said. He doubled-up, groaning, and fell against his companions.

'Now get out,' she said. 'Go on, *go*. Before I cripple the lot of you.'

The drunk tried to straighten.

'Don't you dare try anything with me!' she said. Supported, cursing, he hobbled out.

The smallest man ran to the stool, climbed up, and switched off the hi-fi. He leapt down, almost fell, and went to the table. He poured himself another whisky, and faced her.

'How many times?' he said. 'How many times have I told you? I can *deal* with the bastards. Don't you believe me?'

'They're getting worse, Ralph?' she said.

'Don't you think I know that?' he said. He pointed the glass, and the whisky rocked over the edge. 'Look at them, look at their faces: not a shred of understanding. Carrion – never a new idea, never a . . .'

The woman in the beaded dress came hurrying, still clutching her loop of tickets.

'What the hell is going on *now*?' she said. 'My God, day after day . . . I've got a man out there, Viv, threatening all kinds . . .'

'He was pestering Ralph,' said Virginia.

'So what's new?' said the woman. She looked at the smallest man as he drank, and then at the decanter. She tried to smile as she turned to us. 'Sorry about this, folks. We're closing for half an hour. Keep your tickets, and come back. See the rest of the fair. Sorry.'

As I passed the tank, the octopus nosed its way along the glass, keeping pace; and in the first booth, one of the heads gave a tremulous cry.

*

Sometime in the night, I heard the mad clarion of a fire-engine, or dreamed I heard it. And in the morning I saw thin wisps of smoke rising from a corner of the fairground.

*

After breakfast I walked over there. It was Sunday, and bells were ringing all over town.

The tent of *The Four Marvels* was no more: burned to the black grass. The sideshows either side were also a clutter of smoking wood and flame-eaten canvas. A few children stood around. There was a throat-catching, acrid smell.

A man was feeding a white horse with grain from a red plastic bucket. He directed me to a cream trailer near the drinking-fountain. Behind the trailer, the two-headed goat ate the summer grass, watched by more children.

I knocked on the trailer door. The paintwork was immaculate, the chrome curving reflected trees. The door opened. The smallest man stood there, unshaven, tired-eyed. He wore a blue dressing-gown over paler blue pyjamas, and his feet were bare. His right hand shook slightly.

'Yes' he said.

I held out the pound.

'I want to give you this.'

'We're not starting a collection,' he said.

'It's yours.'

His face cleared.

'Oh, that,' he said: 'Satie.'

'Yes.'

Behind me a child said:

'Look, there he is.'

The smallest man stepped back.

'Come in, please,' he said; and shut the door behind me.

16

The trailer was a miniature home. I felt enormous.

'Sit down,' he said, and I sat on the divan by the back window.

'Was it the drunk?' I said.

'Who else?' He brought the bottle and two glasses. 'Nothing will happen: travelling people . . . You'll join me?'

I never drank that early – it fuzzed the day – but I said yes. He sat cross-legged in a pink silk chair. Holding the glass, I tried to give him the pound.

'You're insulting me, you know that?' he said. 'Put it away. Cheers.'

'Cheers,' I said. The whisky burned away the taste of breakfast. 'Did you save the hi-fi?'

He nodded to a closed cabinet.

'I never leave it in the tent: it means too much to me. The octopus died – of fright, probably.'

'What will you do now?' I said.

'How tall are you?'

'Six two.'

'And what do you do?'

'I teach.'

'What subject?'

'Music.'

'Never a pound more easily earned,' he said. 'Tall, and musical: you're lucky. Do you play?'

'Piano,' I said. 'And you?'

And realised the futility of the question: his fingers spanning a toy keyboard, no more.

His tongue found his dry lips.

What the hell! I thought: *we all have our troubles*. I held out the empty glass.

*

The trailer was becoming over-warm. I loosened my tie. He sat like a small, sweating Buddha. The door opened. The bearded lady stood on the step; behind her, smiling children. She looked fresh and clean, ready for the day, a new beginning.

'How many times have I told you to knock, woman?' he said, craning his head to her; and even I heard the whisky in the words.

She closed the door on the stretching kids, and sat near him.

17

Sunlight through the net curtains woke the auburn hairs in her beard. Were there men who loved bearded women . . .?

'This won't help, Ralph,' she said, and there was a deep sadness.

'It always does,' he said. 'Help yourself.'

'No, thank you,' she said: 'I'm going to church with Ned and Alice.'

'Christ!' he said. 'Say one for me. Oh, excuse me, you haven't met Satie, have you?'

I stood up and banged my head.

She shook my hand, but did not like me.

'You shouldn't let him,' she said. 'When he's sober, he's . . .'

'Pitiable,' he said. 'Go to church, you stupid woman. Let them all look at you, all through the service.'

She stood up.

'That's what we're here for, isn't it, Ralph? So they can look?'

'Not me,' he said. 'Go.'

'I'll see you later. We'll fix something up.'

'We'll fix nothing,' he said. 'It's finished. Act of God. That drunk was John the Baptist. Thank him for me. I'm out.'

She looked at me.

'I would have thought better of you,' she said.

'Go!' said the smallest man.

*

The morning passed, the bells fell silent. The bottle was almost empty.

'Wasn't there a book called that?: *A Rage To Live?*' he said. 'I seem to remember . . .

'My parents were normal, you know that? And I came along. Perfect in every detail. Ha. You can imagine my adolescence: we'll draw a veil. My parents loved me. Amazing, isn't it? Gone now. Maudlin, yes? Let's not . . .

'Who are your favourite composers? Mahler tears me apart. Debussy . . . sparkles.

'Ever thought of life from my level? Legs and wheels.

'I love women.' His hand carved the air. 'I've had a few offers. Cranks. Some dream of a man-child. Fondling. Perverse, really. I ran like the wind, or a wind with short legs. Ha.

'More? I don't think I will, either. Tastes like oil, in the end . . .

'Read much, do you? I never stop. That, and music. My two pillars. You like Whitman? I love Wallace Stevens: like walking through a scented landscape. Anything that takes me out of this bastard world. Forgive my profanity: Virginia never swears, but she can take a man's balls away.

'If I *do* something, I could survive. Something . . . spectacular. Two foot of shit, that's me. No, it's true. What do you see?: a little man, hurrying. But I contain . . . giants. Flamboyant? – well, why not? Let's be flamboyant. Let's be . . . outsize.

'Can you honestly imagine me doing anything else? Is there anything at all? – great composer, artist, poet? Do you like Sisley? I swear those trees of his *move*. Paints fresh air, that man . . .

'Oh Jesus, isn't it awful being chained like this? Held-down. I could burst, you know that?

'Virginia has a house in New Malden. Know New Malden? Near Surbiton, on the Portsmouth line. Little house, little garden. All the lawns the same size. Retired bank-managers cutting the grass on Sunday mornings. Car-cleaning by numbers, right? Good morning to the little man who lives with the bearded lady. Christ! can you *imagine?* Good Christian woman – loves God in spite of . . .

'But what else, Satie, eh? Another fair? One of Snow White's friends?

'Do you think I'll be a giant in the next life? *The Tallest Man In The World* – how's that for reward?'

*

Someone was at the door.

'Come in, damn you!' he shouted.

The first policeman wrinkled his nose at the hot, whisky air. Behind the other, the day blazed green.

'Mr Smith?' said the first.

'Ralph Smith, yes,' said the smallest man.

'Miss Virginia Temple is not available . . .'

'Gone to church,' said the smallest man: 'where we should all be, praising . . . Can I help you, officer?'

'A few questions, if you don't mind.'

19

I stood up, and banged my head again.

'I'll go now,' I said. 'All the best.'

His hand disappeared in mine.

'The best is yet to be: don't they say that?' he said. 'Keep up the good work, Satie.'

The air cooled my face. Then the sun struck down.

I found a shaded place on the Heath. Lay down in long grass; and birds and the far cries of children drowned me in sleep.

*

I opened my eyes. Above me, leaves moved, releasing darts of sun.

*

I thought of dead Mahler, whose works tore apart the smallest man in the world . . .

I thought of Whitman, lounging, a spear of grass between his lips . . .

I thought of Stevens, walking between parasols and blackbirds . . .

Of Cicero among the cypresses . . .

I thought of Sisley, his easel shifting in the wind off the sea, painting air . . .

I thought of my desire to die.

*

And knew I could not.

THE TROUBLE WITH NATHAN

One morning, alone in the house, his hand drawn back to send another piece of bread through the open french windows to the sparrows, his heart lurched in his body.

Still holding the bread, he went to the telephone.

'Yes?'

'Mr Moss?'

'Yes.'

'Andrews, Divisional Office. Can you help us?'

He looked at his mother's clock on the mantelpiece: the china child bouncing up and down in its silver-corded swing.

'Where?'

'Ashdown Comprehensive, Ashborn Avenue. Teacher there gone sick. English master. Know the school?'

'I've . . . heard of it. I've never been there.'

'You'll be all right. Good Headmaster. Mr Pilling. You'll go along, will you?'

Heart racing, sweat in his armpits, he swallowed.

'Now?'

'Yes. If you could. They're a bit short. Okay?'

'Yes . . . I suppose so. For how long?'

'I don't know. Depends on the other chap. Week, two weeks . . . That all right?'

'Yes.'

'Fine. I'll tell Mr Pilling you're on your way. Goodbye, Mr Moss. And thanks.'

He ate the piece of bread himself, distractedly, as he poured himself another cup of tea; found it too hot, added milk, and drank it thirstily. He looked around the room as though for some image of support; returning to the clock, the ever-smiling child.

He shrugged into his coat, and left the house.

*

He entered the deserted playground at ten twenty-five, and began to cross the grey tarmac.

A boy was coming out of the toilets near the shed.

'The Headmaster, please?' said Harold Moss.

The large pink bubble popped, and left the remains of a mask about the boy's lips. He sucked back the gum.

'I'll take you there. You a parent?'

'No.'

They began to climb the steps.

'Student?'

'No.'

'Inspector?'

'You ask a lot of questions.'

They were now on the first floor. The shiny brown tiles.

'Teacher, then?'

'Yes.'

The boy pointed to a green door.

'That's Pilling's pad. See yer.'

Harold settled himself into his clothes, and knocked.

'Yes?' said a voice.

Harold turned the brass handle, and entered.

The Headmaster looked up, defensively.

'I'm Harold Moss. The . . . supply?'

The Headmaster relaxed. Smiled. Stood up, and held out his hand.

'Good to see you. Come along.'

'Don't you want to . . . take any particulars? Discuss . . .?'

'We can do that later, can't we?' He stood aside so that Harold could go before him. 'The class is waiting.'

They went up to the second floor. Crossed a small hall. A soft drone of voices came from the classrooms.

'They're not a bad bunch of boys,' said the Headmaster. 'Experienced, are you?'

'Yes,' said Harold. 'How . . . how many are there?'

'In 4C? Thirty-six.'

'And their English master . . .?'

'Sad case,' said the Headmaster. 'They'll be your own form, virtually. You'll have them for most of the time, aside from practical subjects. Mostly remedial work. If you take everything from the point of view of football – you'll be all right.'

He stopped outside a door. There was silence behind the green curtain covering the glass. The Headmaster looked at him.

'Get a boy called Nathan on your side from the beginning, and you're home and dry.'

He opened the door.

*

When the Headmaster had gone, making no introduction, and taking a white-faced middle-aged woman with him, Harold took off his coat, hung it on the hook at the side of the cupboard, and stood before the silent rows. Thirty-six teenage boys waiting, silently. Thirty-six personalities to interest, and subdue. The customary battlefield.

'Which one of you is Nathan?' he said.

A slim, dark, good-looking boy in the centre of the front row smiled, and put up his hand.

'Here, sir.'

'Right,' said Harold. He wiped his hands, put the handkerchief back in his top pocket, and picked up a piece of chalk. He turned his back on the class and wrote on the board. And as he wrote, he waited. But there was not a sound. Not even the scrape of a chair. He turned back to their intent and half-smiling faces.

'That is my name,' he said. 'Moss. *Mr* Moss. And I've been teaching for ten years. So I know my job. I have handled boys tougher than you; and I want you to remember that *I* am in charge of this class, no one else. What I say, goes. Right?'

There was no response. Then Nathan spoke.

'Yes, sir.'

'Good. Just so long as we understand each other. From the beginning. Start as we mean to go on. Now, have you a copy of your timetable?'

'On the wall behind you, sir,' said Nathan.

Harold smiled at the boy.

'Thank you.' He took the stiff card from its hook.

'Now, shall we go through it together . . .?'

*

When the bell rang for break, they waited. Silently.

'Right,' said Harold. 'Stand.'

They filed out without a sound; Nathan last.

'Shall I show you the staffroom, sir?' he said.

'Yes. Thank you.'

The rest of the classes roared across the hall, making for the stairs.

'Live near here, sir?' said Nathan. He held the hall door open for Harold.

'Not far,' said Harold. 'Battersea. Archer's Road.'

'Oh, near the river, sir?'

'Yes.'

'Nice.'

They went up two flights of stairs.

'This is it, sir.'

'Thank you, Nathan.'

The room was the same room he had entered in school after school. Tables. Piles of exercise books. A sense of desperation.

'Sugar?' said a thin man.

'Yes, thanks. Two, please.'

'Harper,' said the man. 'Maths.'

'Oh, I'm Moss. Thank you. On supply. Taking 4C.'

The man leaned against the window and sipped his tea.

'Are you now? You've met Nathan then?'

'Yes.'

Harper nodded.

'Nice lad.'

*

The end of the morning came. They filed out again; and as quietly.

'Staying for school dinner, sir?' said Nathan.

'No,' said Harold, getting into his coat. 'I . . . like to eat out of school.'

'Don't blame you, sir,' said Nathan. 'I *have* to stay, worse luck. Mum and Dad out all day. I go to the chip shop sometimes. Do you want to know a good café, sir?'

'Yes, well, I suppose . . .'

'Baroni's, sir. Not far from here. Only takes five minutes. End of the Avenue. That end. Turn right, first right – and you're there. Cheap, too.'

'Thank you, Nathan, I'll . . . try it.'

And it was a good café: clean, with good plain food; and cheap. The girl gave him his change. She was tall with milky skin and proud breasts.

'See you again,' she said.

'Yes,' said Harold. 'Tomorrow.'

Nathan was in the playground, talking to two other members of 4C.

'Good afternoon, sir,' he said. 'Did you try Baroni's?'

'Yes,' said Harold. 'Very nice, Nathan. Thank you for telling me.'

'See Susie?' said another boy.

Nathan looked at him, and the boy coloured.

'The waitress, sir,' he said. 'Susie.'

'Oh, is that her name?' said Harold. 'Yes.'

*

He marked the register: everyone was present. The afternoon consisted of two periods: history and English. The history master was absent.

'What have you been studying?' said Harold.

'Civil War, sir,' said Nathan. 'It's in the books, sir. Mr Warren was on page . . . ninety-eight, sir.'

'What happened to your English teacher?' said Harold.

The boys were very still. They looked at Nathan.

'Mr Peters, sir? Nothing much. Just . . . ill. I don't think he'll be coming back, sir. Anyway, we'd rather have you, sir.'

The other boys nodded.

'I don't know about that,' said Harold. 'We must see . . . how we get on.'

And they got on very well. Harold was amazed at their quietness, their industry; and, at the end of the day, touched by their obvious reluctance to go home. But go home at last they did, giving cheerful good-nights and thank-yous. Nathan last, as usual.

'See you tomorrow, sir,' he said. 'Best teacher we've ever had, sir.'

Harold had never felt less tired at the end of a teaching day. Riding home in the bus, the unopened newspaper on his lap, he looked at the world through fresh, wide-awake eyes. Perhaps, at last, he had found it: that ease of communication, which had so long eluded him. Perhaps this was the beginning. After all, despite past exhaustion and fear, he had always liked young people. Yes. He began to whistle, softly. And opened the paper.

*

He was early the next morning: wanting to prepare the first lessons; go through a few textbooks in the cupboard. But Nathan was there before him, sitting on the steps.

'Morning, sir. Want any help?'

'No, I don't think so, Nathan. Thank you.' He looked around the deserted playground. 'Are you always the first?'

'Nothing much to do at home, sir.'

Harold went up to the classroom, prepared his lessons, and sat at his desk with the open register before him as the whistle sounded below and the shouting ceased.

He waited, a half-smile playing about his lips. *His* form were coming. *His* class. the quiet ones: ones he could control.

They came in like an avalanche. An avalanche of noise: shouts, stamping of feet, whistles. At first he thought they could not be aware of him. But, seeing him sitting there, shocked, open-mouthed, they redoubled the volume, flinging themselves about the room, knocking over chairs, books. A glass vase fell from a window-ledge and smashed. Harold, the old sick fear returning, began to stand.

Then Nathan entered.

And, as if a switch had been pulled, the noise abruptly ended.

'Okay,' said Nathan: 'that's enough.' He looked at the splinters of winking glass. 'Who did that?'

'I did, Nathan,' said one of the boys. 'Sorry.'

'Go and get a dustpan and brush,' said Nathan. 'Clear it up.' He turned to Harold. 'Sorry about the noise, sir.'

Harold gathered himself together.

'Well . . . thank you, Nathan.'

Nathan smiled.

'Any time, sir,' he said.

Harold had two other forms for English that morning, and survived. His own form, when they returned, were quiet and attentive, and worked well. He looked at Nathan often as the day progressed: as a disciple looks at a god.

Crossing the playground at lunchtime, he found the boy walking beside him.

'Mind if I join you at Baroni's today, sir?' said Nathan. 'I feel like a change.'

'Well, I . . . I suppose so. Yes, come along.'

When they entered the café, the girl smiled at Harold.

'Hallo, sir,' she said.

'Hi, Susie,' said Nathan. They sat down. Nathan leaned forward. 'Nice pair there, sir.'

Harold was silent, head down, inspecting the menu.

'I'll have what I had yesterday, please,' he said, when the girl came back.

'The lamb,' she said. 'And you?'

'I'll have the same as my teacher.'

'You his teacher?' she said. 'I wouldn't wish him on anyone.'

She went to the counter. Nathan watched her go.

'Not all that bad, am I, sir?'

'On the contrary . . .' said Harold.

Nathan smiled.

'Thank you, sir.'

After the meal, they had coffee. Pleasantly full, pleased with life, Harold watched as Nathan took out a pack of cigarettes.

'Sir?'

'No, thank you. I don't smoke. And I don't think you should, either. Did you have those in school?'

'Cancer, I know, sir.' He lit up, and sucked the smoke down. It appeared, lazily, from his nose. 'Sure you won't have one?'

'No, thank you.'

Nathan leaned forward; and now, close to, Harold was conscious for the first time how rodent-like the boy's face was. Predatory.

27

'I shall want forty of these a day,' said Nathan.

'*Shall*?' said Harold.

'From you, sir.'

A strange feeling ran through Harold: his blood melting, yet freezing. He smiled.

'What do you mean?'

'And a tenner. A week.'

'I don't know what you mean.'

'Seven, Archer's Road. Right?'

'Yes,' said Harold. 'That's my address.'

'Mother dead, right? Married couple in the first-floor flat? Nice little house, yours. We were round there last night . . .'

'*Who* were?'

'Me and the lads. The 4C Boys.'

'I didn't see . . .'

'Nice windows. Not smashed.'

'I don't understand you.'

Nathan leaned back, and the smoke seemed to follow him.

'Remember how noisy it was, this morning? How it all went quiet when I came in? Well, you've got a choice, Mr Moss. If you want it quiet all the time – *and* no windows broken – it's forty fags a day and a tenner a week. I have to think of the lads. Cost of living.'

'You mean: Mr Peters . . .'

'Ah, you get the message. He won't be back.'

'I can't do it. I won't do it.'

'Look, Mr Moss, you want a nice quiet class. You have to be there, *we* have to be there. Why don't we work together? We could make it cushy for you, nice as pie. Forty a day and a tenner. Not going to break you, is it? You get a good rate, you supply teachers . . .'

'I'll see Mr Pilling . . .'

'Your word against mine, Mr Moss. They like me there. Head Boy next year: I can see it coming. Very willing, I am. Always available. First in the morning, last at night. And it *is* a nice house in a quiet street; nice married couple, paying you rent, not wanting to be . . . disturbed?'

Harold was silent.

'Thirty-six of us, remember?' said Nathan. He smiled. 'Needn't pay this week. Let you off. Start next Monday, yes?'

Silence.

'Have another coffee, Mr Moss. Susie! Two more coffees, love. And Mr Moss wants the bill. He's treating me.'

*

And so they began: those days of quietness in the class; those Monday walks to Baroni's, when the cigarettes and the money were handed over. Long, tense, silent days leading to the peaceful islands of the weekend.

But even these began to be disturbed when, one Sunday, sunk in the armchair watching TV, the couple away until Monday, he heard tapping at the window, and turned to see three grinning faces pressed against the glass.

Nathan, in the centre, tapped harder, and mouthed *Cup of tea?*

They came in, all bristling life and cigarette-smoke, and overpowered the room. They lolled in his chairs.

'What you watching?' said Jackson.

'It's about Australia,' said Harold, 'The . . . '

'Kettle, Mr Moss?' said Nathan.

When he came back, they had switched channels to yesterday's big match. The crowd roared, Jackson was out of his chair and prowling around. Reaching the mantelpiece, he fingered the clock.

'Don't touch that!' Harold shouted.

But the damage was done: the swing clattered on one silver chord, the child spinning.

'Clumsy bastard you are, Jacko,' said Nathan. 'Say you're sorry.'

'Sorry, Mr Moss,' said Jackson, smiling.

*

On the Monday of the fifth week, they sat together in Baroni's.

'We'll have the steak-and-kidney pie, with new potatoes and peas, followed by apple-pie and custard; and coffee,' said Nathan. 'All right, Harold?'

'You allow him to call you Harold?' said Susie. 'No wonder schools have got no discipline.'

'Go and get dinner, luscious', said Nathan.

She shook her head.

'It's all wrong,' she said.

'You're not eating, Harold,' said Nathan, later.

Harold pushed his plate away.

'I can't go on', he said.

'It's good grub.'

'You know what I mean', said Harold.

Nathan's head came up.

'Forty and the tenner,' he said. 'You got them?'

'No.'

'There's a shop on the corner and a bank further down.'

'No,' said Harold. He felt courage glow like a flame. 'No. Not any more, Nathan.' He stood up. 'And you pay for your own lunch.'

He went to the counter.

'You all right?' said Susie.

'I'm in a hurry,' said Harold. 'Just mine today.'

'About time,' she said. 'Horrible little bugger, he is.'

'Yes,' said Harold.

He went straight back to the school, cleared his desk, and waited.

*

They came in quietly and sat down. Harold called the register. Everyone was present. He closed the thin book and folded his hands on the desk.

'I've been doing some thinking,' he said.

Someone coughed loudly at the back.

Harold swallowed the dry stone in his throat.

'This is my last day here,' he said.

'We'll come round your house tonight,' said Nathan.

'Smash your windows,' said another.

'I shall go to the police immediately after school,' said Nathan.

'We'll sort you out one night,' said Jackson.

'No,' said Nathan, quietly. '*We* won't. We'll get someone to do it for us. We'll be in the clear. You can't touch us, Harold. We'll get someone to break in and smash everything you've got: that stupid baby clock, all those crappy pictures . . . '

Harold's fraying control broke. He launched himself from behind his table and grabbed the boy. He wrapped his hands around Nathan's throat, lifted him with a strength he never knew he possessed, and threw him across the room. The boy hit a low cupboard, fell, and in falling struck the corner of a desk. Harold picked him up by his shirt collar. The material ripped. Nathan was thrown again.

'Stop it!' cried Jackson. 'You're killin' him!'

'I'll . . . kill him,' said Harold. He made to make another attack. Then he saw the blood.

*

Harold sat in the Headmaster's study.

'What got into you, man?' said Pilling. 'One of the best behaved . . . '

'I want to go home,' said Nathan.

'I think you'd better,' said the Headmaster.

'I won't be coming back.'

'No, you will *not*. I can't understand it. The boy may have a fractured skull. Nathan, of all boys. Who knows what damage you've done.'

Harold stood, wearily.

'Goodbye, Mr Pilling.'

'I'll be in touch with you, Mr Moss. It won't rest here, you know that. You'd better be ready with some explanation.'

Harold walked all the way home. He made a pot of tea; watched the smiling child jog in the repaired swing; listened to the radio. He was still there when night came: listening in the dark. Soft laughter came from the flat above. Movement.

He went to bed, and fell immediately asleep.

*

The nightmare began.

He saw Nathan's face, running with blood, the small rat-eyes filling. The teeth changing colour. He saw a naked Susie leaning her white breasts, and the breasts opened like red flowers and he was engulfed with evil-smelling liquid. He saw Nathan's funeral, the sharp, cold-pinched faces of the rest of the class. And then it was the trial, and the judge was Mr Pilling; the jurors every child

31

Harold had ever taught: all the remembered faces. Sentenced to death, he approached the hangman. The rope was placed about his neck. Tightening . . .

And then his mother appeared, and he was home once again, and she was sitting on the end of the bed, wiping away the sweat. He became calm.

And woke.

Sunlight filled the room. A sparrow chittered in the eaves.

'Oh thank God,' he said. 'Thank God.'

He felt a movement at the end of the bed.

'Mother?' he said.

Nathan, a bloodied bandage about his forehead, smiled with his small red rat-like teeth.

'It's me, Harold,' he said. 'I've come to stay.'

Afternoon School

'Is there a clean shirt?' he said, standing in his underwear at the top of the stairs.

She came out of the living-room.

'You look like something out of mail-order,' she said.

'How would you know? Is there a clean shirt?'

'You had a clean one on this morning. He's not going to examine you, is he?'

'I don't know what he's going to do. *Is* there a clean shirt?'

'There's one in the airing-cupboard,' she said.

He went back into the bathroom and opened the airing-cupboard door. The white shirt stirred in warm air. He took it off the hanger, put it on; and swore.

She was sorting out her library books.

'What's the matter now?' she said.

He held out the limp white sleeve.

'No button,' he said.

'It's not the end of the world,' she said. 'Go and get your trousers on.'

'Why your best suit?' she said, when he came back. She lowered her head to position the button, and pushed the needle through. The white thread ran, and tightened. 'Two shirts in one day; best suit – you haven't got a mistress, have you?'

'I have, I'm afraid,' he said. 'Miss Atkins and I have a love-nest on Market Street.'

She laughed at the picture of him making love to his thin, plain secretary: thin limbs askew, little squeals of delight mixed with fear.

'What's that smell?' she said.

'It's the after-shave Robin bought me for Christmas. It's called *Assegai*. It brings women to their knees.'

'And water-buffalo,' she said. She snapped the thread free, and

33

looked up at him. 'What did Forster actually *say*?'

'It wasn't Forster. It was the young chap: Rigg. Forster's off for a week.'

'Can't it wait until he gets back?'

He smoothed his tie and put on his jacket.

'Apparently not.'

'George,' she said: 'you're telling me everything, aren't you?'

'No', he said; 'but I will. No need to take me all the way: drop me off at the library. I'll walk the rest.'

'When did you last read a book?' she said.

'You read enough for both of us.'

'There are some good biographies, these days . . . '

'Grace,' he said, lifting a hand: 'spare me.'

*

On the road outside the library, gloved hands on the wheel, she looked out at him.

'Will you be going back to the office, after?'

'I may look in.'

'It was a silly question. *May* look in! Why don't we go mad and meet for tea at Holland's? Say, three-thirty?'

'No, I'll see you back at home: five-ish.'

'I may be a little late. I promised to see Louise.'

'Okay,' he said. 'Take care.' And watched her drive off to the car-park.

He began to walk.

He had not gone ten paces up the hill, when a woman, coming down, said:

'Good afternoon, Mr Smethurst.'

He raised his hat.

'Good afternoon.'

He had no idea who she was. But everyone knew him – his progress marked by nods and smiles.

At the top of the hill, he turned right. He had lived in the town for forty years, and knew every brick, every tree. *Thompson's Garage, the Rex Cinema, the Parade, Stuffed Owl Antiques, the church.* A class of schoolchildren were sitting on the grass beyond the gravestones, listening to a teacher. *The Chocolate Box, Field's Delicatessen, the Midland Bank, the White Hart Hotel* – and then

his own wide windows filled with pictures of desirable prop-
erties: *Smethurst's The Estate Agents*. The top photograph on the
second column was crooked. He glanced in at the entrance as he
passed. Peggy, the switchboard-operator, had a paperback propped against her lines. Note number two.

He crossed by the post-office, around the car-showrooms, and
entered Duval Avenue. Three houses had his distinctive *For Sale*
signs in their front gardens. A little ahead of the doctors' surgery
was that bastard Whittaker's property: the continuing legal
hassle, pin-pricks though they were, still rankled . . .

The receptionist smiled a little too brightly, he thought.

'Good afternoon, Mr Smethurst,' she said. 'Doctor Rigg will
see you next.'

The waiting-room was very warm. He loosened his coat. An
old man cleared his lungs and spat into a handkerchief. A child
ran back and forth, watched by its young mother. Outside the
window, sunlight glinted on an airliner.

A voice spoke in the speakers above the door.

'Mr Smethurst.'

*

Rigg stood up from behind his table. Behind him leaves touched
the window, made the room green. He was young and tired, but
made a show of energy, his handshake powerful enough to feel
the bone.

'We haven't met before.'

'No.'

'Sit down, please.'

Smethurst liked order. Forster's table was always cluttered;
this man's was bare, save for a large envelope.

Rigg sat down.

'Beautiful day,' he said.

'Yes.'

'How's the estate business?'

'Looking for a house?'

Rigg smiled.

'I may do.'

They both heard the child run down the corridor.

'Patsy, *wait!*'

A door closed.

'Well?' said Smethurst.

'Doctor Forster sent you for tests . . . '

'Yes.'

'Symptoms?'

'Extreme tiredness. Lethargy. Falling asleep during the day: not like me.'

'Any unusual bleeding?'

'Bleeding? No. In what way?'

'Pressing through the skin. Slight knocks . . . '

'No.' He looked at the envelope. 'Is that the result?'

'Yes.' Rigg opened it and took out two sheets of typed paper. 'Have you ever been exposed to radiation? Of any kind?'

'No.'

'Not in the army? The Services?'

'I'm not that old.'

'Always been in the estate business?'

'In one way or another: yes. Will you show me that?'

'No.' Rigg put the papers under the envelope. 'We haven't met before, and . . . '

'If it couldn't wait for Forster, it must be serious.'

'It is.'

'Tell me.'

Rigg looked at him.

'You have leukaemia, Mr Smethurst.'

All the objects in the room seemed to separate themselves from their surroundings: to exist in individual, well-defined shapes.

'A cancer of the blood,' said Rigg.

'I know what leukaemia is,' said Smethurst. 'There's no history . . . '

'There doesn't have to be.'

'How bad?'

'We want you to go into the Elizabeth Allen Hospital tonight.'

'How bad?'

'The fact that we want you . . . '

'I want to see those papers.'

'I don't think that's advisable.'

Smethurst held out his hand, and was surprised at its steadiness.

36

'Are we children?' he said.

'It's just a mass of figures, Mr Smethurst. I can tell you what it says: that you have a dangerously high white-cell count . . . '

'I respected Forster,' said Smethurst.

Rigg took the sheets from under the envelope.

'Thank you,' said Smethurst.

A slip of paper was stapled to the first sheet:

Mr George Smethurst, a fifty-five-year-old businessman, with no previous serious medical history, has complained of . . .

He read no further, and lifted the slip. The tests were detailed: figures and strange names. He turned to the second page. At the bottom, other words leapt:

Diagnosis: Acute myelogenous leukaemia.

Prognosis: Terminal.

*

The *T* of *Terminal* was darker than the rest of the word, as though the typist had decided to ram home the truth, and then came compassion.

As the pause grew into silence, Rigg said:

'You *did* insist.'

'Yes. It's always best to know.'

'We are all terminal, Mr Smethurst.'

'But some are more terminal than others, right?' He looked at the sharp shape of the doctor's head against the window. 'How long?'

'Let's wait until we get you into hospital . . . '

'How long?'

Rigg spread his hands.

'It differs with each individual. Some . . . '

'At the outside, then.'

'A lot can be done. Drugs. There's a gradual weakening . . . All right. You could have months; you could have six weeks. So you see the urgency. Can you arrange to be at the hospital by six? I've already booked a bed. You'll be in Grantley Ward.'

'Grantley. Right.' He put the papers on the table. 'Is there anything else?'

'Forster will pop in and see you later in the week, I'm sure.'

'Where is he?' said Smethurst.

37

'Corfu,' said Rigg. He motioned to a steel cabinet. 'I've got some brandy in there . . . '

'No thank you,' he said. He stood up.

'Will you tell your wife and son?' said Rigg: 'I mean – how serious . . . ?'

'You mean there's an alternative?' said Smethurst.

*

The receptionist smiled brightly:

'Goodbye, Mr Smethurst.'

He nodded, but said nothing.

Without registering how he got there, he found himself outside the delicatessen. He had blindly passed his own windows for the first time in sixteen years. Custom made him start to go back; then he halted on the pavement. There seemed no need, now. He walked on, the possessor of a clear, cold fact that was changing his life, whilst the rest of the untouched world went about its business.

By the time he reached the church, the familiar afternoon weariness had returned: now he knew why. He thought of the pale blood shuttling through his veins: how it had pumped rich and red last year, when he had gashed his hand on one of Whittaker's vandalised windows. Was the disease present then? How long did leukaemia . . . ?

There were benches in the churchyard. The path was made of large flat gravestones, bearing eighteenth-century dates. He walked on names and ages: father, mother, child. *1976. Andrew Cox. Aged 34. Beloved husband of . . .*

He sat on a bench in the sun. He took off his hat, unbuttoned his coat, and spread his arms either side on the warm wood.

To be dead within six weeks. To be at one with those on whose lost names he had trod. To be finished, at fifty-five. *Andrew Cox: 34*. At least he had had twenty-one years more – but what had he done with them? He had never been introspective, like Robin. Not in his nature; never had the time. *Smethurst Estate Agent*: that was his life. All those years, sleeping and waking: farmhouses, luxury apartments, cottages, mansions; contracts, surveyors, accountants, auctions. He realised now that the business owned *him*, rather than the reverse. He had drawn it around

38

himself like a cloak, a favourite blanket, which nothing could penetrate. He had no other interests: it was Grace and Robin who took holidays; Forster sunning himself in Corfu . . . He had lived and breathed the dust of leases; and now his own lease was up, and there was no renewal.

Warm air, bearing the scent of grass and treebark, eddied about his face. He was conscious of his own, never-to-come-again individuality – George Smethurst, *me* – a living man, on a bench in the sun. What would those who hung in the earth below him give for another six weeks, even a second of this air!

The afternoon school was still in progress on the grass beyond the gravestones. Children running in some sort of game. Laughter, flash of limbs. Feet on grass, then on stone . . .

As if his eyes were peeled, he saw the white bones of the children and the white bones of the dead over which they ran. He saw the world riddled with little pockets of space into which bones were tidily slotted. These children who laughed would have their own names carved; other children, perhaps their own, would have their running time – as this was his: soon to halt and stumble, to be lifted by others, set tidily . . . down. He knew he had wasted his life. He had provided shelter for thousands, and now nothing could shelter him.

The day, every day, was a miracle. He knew that now. Now that he was leaving it, the Earth was a treasure-house. Perhaps he would go on: the soul winging . . . But the Earth was good enough for him: good food, and the slide of a woman under his hands . . . Heaven would be nothing but boring: eternally singing hosannahs to a self-satisfied Creator. Not that he believed in any of that . . .

Out of the past, from some forgotten lesson, a line came: *None I think do there embrace* . . . And it was true.

Six weeks. *A gradual weakening* . . .

He would not go to the hospital. He had a horror of being at the mercy of others, of tubes and needles and the clotted snoring of dying men. He would never return to the office. He had a few thousand in the deposit account. He would pack a lifetime into those six weeks. Doing what . . . ?

A child came running by, and he marked its fragility. People passed on the other side of the low wall: he heard a snatch of conversation, human words. Did everyone *know* how transitory everything was?

He would go on a cruise, with Grace. He would soak up the sun on some shining deck, listening to waves against a white bow. He would see Egyptian tombs and Grecian temples; watch dancers in Bali; take a look at Ayers Rock. He would read books in shadowed deckchairs; listen to music in some great concert hall . . . And then he would die – where it did not matter – beach, hotel-room; in a rowing-boat on a still lake; in a white ward watched by nuns.

Sitting there, he was astonished. Words on a piece of paper had liberated him. He had discovered a way of looking at the world: this casually-accepted, sometime grudgingly-borne existence.

He looked down at his shoes. They rested on another gravestone. The curved leather half-hid a name. *Ge* . . . Was it his own? *Gerrard Withington. Aged 81.* Lucky old Gerrard.

The teacher was calling the children to her. The church clock struck three-thirty. Afternoon school was over. Time to go home.

*

Striding out, he found all weariness had gone. Perhaps that was the answer: faced with the prospect of your own extinction, you marshalled all your forces, re-vitalised the blood, made it richer. He almost ran.

When he got home the house had changed, as had the day. Possessions he had ignored for years: vases, paperweights, wall-plates, porcelain figures – they were seen afresh, as if newly made. The hyacinths in the window-seat bristled with life. Even his coat, as he hung it in the hall-closet, had a thicker, warmer texture.

He went into the living-room. He would waste no time. He dialled the number.

'Hallo, Louise? George. Is Grace there? She was going to call on you. Will you ask her to phone me, when she gets there? No, at home. Yes. Fine, thanks. And you? Good. Thanks, Louise.'

There was a mirror above the telephone. He looked at himself. The swift walk had coloured his cheeks. The face of a dying man? Nonsense.

He was checking through his last bank statements, when the phone rang. He used the one in his study.

'Grace?' he said.

There was the slightest of pauses.

'Mr Smethurst?'

Yes.'

Another pause.

'Do you have a chair handy?'

'What?'

'Could you sit down for a moment?'

'I am sitting down. Who is this?'

'It's Richard Rigg, Mr Smethurst.' Pause. 'Look, I'm terribly sorry about this. I've just had a panic-stricken call from the Elizabeth Allen. There's been a most terrible mistake. Some stupid cow of a technician clipped your name to the wrong findings.' Slight laugh. 'You haven't started making a will, have you?'

Smethurst looked through the window, but did not see the view.

'What are you trying to tell me?'

'You're clear, Mr Smethurst. Your blood's fine. Years ahead of you. Just a little exhaustion, that's all. Gets to all of us. Take a holiday. Rest more. Find another interest . . .' Silence. A troubled voice. 'Are you there?'

'Yes.'

'Bit of a shaker, I know. I'm sorry. But it has its good side. You must let me buy you a lunch some time. Discuss houses . . . I hope they boot the silly bitch out. You're a healthy man, Mr Smethurst. Be grateful. Are you there?'

'Still here, Mr Rigg.'

'You'll accept my apologies . . . ?'

'Accepted.'

'Thank you. Goodbye.'

'Goodbye.'

*

Now the view appeared: the usual trees, roofs, TV aerials, wires . . .

The years stretched ahead.

The telephone rang again. It was still warm.

'Hallo,' he said, and fire had gone from him.

41

'Mr Smethurst?'

'Yes.'

'It's Stanford, sir. At the office.'

'Yes, Stanford.'

'I'm afraid I'm having a spot of bother here, sir . . . '

'In what way?'

There was a clattering sound.

'Smethurst?' The name was a shout. 'This is Whittaker. I'm here with my solicitor. I want this settled once and for all. *Now.* *Today.* I'm fed up dealing with your underlings. If you're not here in fifteen minutes, I'm taking you to court. You understand that?'

Smethurst shifted inside his clothes.

'Let me speak to Stanford.'

'Are you going to be . . . '

'Stanford, Mr Whittaker, please.'

'Yes, sir?'

Smethurst chose his words with care and pleasure.

'Stanford, tell that ignorant bastard and his equally ignorant solicitor that I will see them in fifteen minutes. Will you do that?'

'Yes, sir. I'm sorry, sir, I could've handled it myself. But . . . '

'Just tell them, Stanford.'

He took his coat from the hall-closet. He opened the front door.

The phone rang in the living-room. He went back, car-keys in his left hand.

She sounded breathless and very anxious.

'Louise asked me to call you. Is everything all right?'

'Yes,' he said. 'Clean bill of health. Thought you'd like to know.'

'Oh, thank God, George!' she said. 'I thought it was something terrible.'

'No,' he said: 'nothing terrible.'

PRIVATE MEADOWS

ONE

He finally arrived. *Be an example to your men.* He was flushed with more than heat. The stories about the woman he had in Heliopolis were true: I had seen her with him in a club banned to Other Ranks; and so, although I was in civilian clothes, I kept out of sight. She was beautiful, and I envied him.

He was a young officer: fresh pink face that would never tan, and a neat sandy moustache.

I pressed the cigarette into the ashtray, stood erect, and saluted him. His was merely a wave: newly risen from that brown body, what were formalities?

'Any messages, Tyler?' he said.

'No, sir,' said the duty-clerk.

'Good. Come through, Corporal.'

'Sir,' I said.

He put his cap and stick on top of a filing-cabinet, and switched on the fan. The blue ribbons lifted lazily, then streamed. He opened the window at the top, and sat behind his desk.

'Stand easy, Mitchell,' he said.

I relaxed. Behind him, through the window, the white tents of the dhobi-wallahs shook in the wind off the Nile.

He sat back and rested his hands on his stomach. He was getting a little plump: tasty morsels buried in mounds of rice, served by his doe-eyed mistress . . .

'I've been watching you, Mitchell. Watching your progress.'

'Sir?'

'How much longer have you got out here?'

'Another year, sir.'

'I go home in six weeks.'

'I know, sir.'

'You're a good man, Mitchell. Discipline without rage. You never seem . . . shaken. I've talked to the CO about you. You're being made Sergeant, as from the first of March.'

'Thank you, sir.'

'You're pleased.' He looked down. 'And I'd like you to take over Barrack Room 3, from that date.'

I saw the reasoning.

'No, thank you, sir.'

He looked up, pretending.

'What?'

'I'd rather not, sir. I'm happy in 8. If being Sergeant means taking over 3, I'll stay Corporal.'

'Stand to attention,' he said. 'Now, listen to me. This is an order, Mitchell, not a request. Sergeant Davies goes home at the end of February: room 3 will be without an NCO. You will be Sergeant from the first of March. You take over from Davies. right? An order, Mitchell.'

'May I speak frankly, sir?'

'When have we never, Mitchell?'

We had never *spoken* at all.

'I don't think I can handle Williams, sir.'

'*Williams*? Of course you can. He goes home at the same time as myself. You can take six weeks of him, can't you?'

'I can't take five minutes of him, sir.'

'See it as a challenge, Mitchell. You handle 8 very well: best kit lay-out; best . . . '

'Because Williams isn't there, sir. All my men are humans.'

He laughed at that.

'It's an order, *Sergeant*. I'll always back you up, if there's any trouble . . . '

'Yes, sir.'

He opened a file.

'And, by the way: a new man is due here on the first. A Private Thomas Meadows. He'll be with you in 3. Another clerk, replacing Everett. See he settles in happily, will you?'

'*Happily*, sir? With Williams?'

'You're still at attention,' he said, playing the officer. 'Don't let me down.'

'No, sir,' I said; and left.

44

Tyler looked up from his papers.

'So?' he said.

'I'm being made Sergeant, from the first.'

'Not before time, Corp.'

'And I'm taking over 3, from Davies.'

His eyes widened.

'You poor sod,' he said.

*

I had five days to get ready, but I knew the word would be around the barracks in an hour. I had to be the first to act.

Davies was sitting on the steps outside 3, cleaning his boots. He was taking great care.

'For the last time,' he said. He held one out at arm's-length. 'Think it'll last till Friday?'

I sat down beside him. The stone was hot.

'If there are no parades,' I said.

'*Parades*? What are they?' He put the boot down, picked up the other, and began using the brush on a toe-cap that was already magnificent. 'An army of pen-pushers.'

I looked down at the grains blown in from the desert.

'Captain Leicester wanted to see me,' I said.

'Not long for him, either,' said Davies. 'You'll be the only one left soon, Jim. You and the shite-hawks.'

'I'm Sergeant from the first week of March,' I said.

He rested the boot on my knee. Sweat moved with his grin.

'Sign on, lad,' he said. 'Do another twelve, and nothing can hold you.'

'And I'm taking over 3, from you.'

'Oh,' he said, and took the boot away. He looked at his squat reflection in the toe-cap. 'That's a blow. For you.'

'Where is he?'

'Gone for a swim.' He looked at me. 'Why?'

'I want to talk to him.'

'Talk to Williams?' he said. 'Why anticipate? Nothing may happen.'

'You know better than that.'

'He's been pretty docile, lately.'

'Only because he's got no money. Come pay-day . . . '

'You want to know the best way to handle him?'

'No'. I stood up. 'I'll buy you a drink tonight.'

'I'll buy *you* one,' he said. 'Congratulations, Jim – I think.'

*

The twelve barrack-rooms framed the ochre-coloured parade-ground on three sides. Once they had been the stables for Arabian stallions. Beyond the stables were the tennis-courts and the swimming-pool, the rich Cairo suburbs – and then the desert.

The light was brutal off the water. I took my sunglasses from my top pocket. The water changed colour: appeared deeper. No drinking was permitted in the camp until six pm. The white circular tables, now blue, held forests of Coke bottles. A few bodies patrolled the pool, but most were sunbathing: dark skin, stretched on long canvas beds, grew darker. Stunned by the heat, they were silent. Behind the slow ripple of the swimmers, I could hear the soft roar of the city's traffic.

He was in the water, making for the far end, taking it easy. Long, powerful strokes. I walked on hot tiles, keeping pace. His hands touched the rail, and he prepared to swim back, bunching his shoulders.

'Williams,' I said.

He shook water out of his eyes, and looked up. Sleek black hair, gleaming shoulders. His right hand wiped his nose.

'What?' he said.

'May I see you for a moment?'

'Ten lengths,' he said. 'I've got two more.'

'I'll be over there,' I said.

He nodded, and struck out. Water splashed my shoes.

I got two Cokes and paper cups, and chose a table with an umbrella. Protected, I took off my sunglasses. Light was still fierce on tiles and water, and I eased my eyes on dusty, wind-stirred palms.

He padded to the table, leaving footprints which dried immediately. Out of the water, he was less impressive: one brown leg looked wasted, as though thinned by a childhood illness. But the hairy chest, glistening with drops, was strong. He rubbed it with a towel. And then that dark face. He sat heavily in the slatted

46

chair. We knew each other, but had rarely exchanged a word. He looked at the Coke.

'I hate that stuff,' he said. 'You know it's full of sugar?'

'What do you like?'

'Milk.'

I laughed.

'It's true,' he said. 'Nothing like a glass of ice-cold milk.'

'When you're in training.'

'When I'm in training.'

I went and got him some milk. It whitened his top lip, and he licked it clean. He burped softly.

'Beautiful,' he said, and had I known him less, I would have found the Welsh lilt charming. His body dry now, he turned the glass in one brown hairy hand. 'What do you want, Corp?'

'You know Davies is leaving on Friday?'

'Me, too, in six weeks,' he said. 'Back home, out of it. A free man.'

'I'm being promoted to Sergeant, and I'm taking over 3.'

The glass stopped turning, and he became watchful.

'Are you now?' he said. 'We'll have to smarten ourselves up.'

'I wanted to have a word with you, before that happens. Just to . . . put you in the picture.'

'You do that, Corp,' he said: 'you put me in the picture.'

'Let's not mince words, Williams . . . '

'Taff,' he said. 'I like to be called Taff. Or Taffy.'

I pretended a strength I did not possess.

'We'll stick to Williams for the moment,' I said. '*You* know what you are, and I know what you are. You've only got six weeks: I want them peaceful.'

'What am I, Corp?' he said. 'Tell me what I am.'

'You're a man who changes with drink,' I said. 'You can't handle it. Yet you go on.'

He lifted the glass.

'I'm on the wagon.'

'Until pay-day,' I said. 'I tell you this, Williams: I'm not Davies. I won't take it. Your feet won't touch the ground. I'll have you. One punch-up, one more smashing of equipment: you'll spend the six weeks at Timsah.'

47

'This is a new you, Corp,' he said. 'This how you keep –
sweet-smelling?'

'I'm just putting things on the line . . . '

'And in the picture,' he said. He finished the milk. 'Have we
done?'

'Do you understand?' I said. 'Once you're back in Cardiff, you
can drink yourself to death. But for six weeks . . . '

'Swansea,' he said. 'Not Cardiff.' He draped the towel around
his neck and got out of the chair. 'Nice talking to you.'

'I'm quiet, until I'm pushed.'

'Ain't we all, Corp?' he said.

*

On Thursday morning, Leicester gave me my new stripes. On
Friday morning I wore them on a newly-cleaned and pressed
uniform. They felt like patches of hard skin. At eleven I drove the
jeep to the station, to pick up Private Meadows.

A number of servicemen got off the train. One – small,
bespectacled, white-fleshed, sweating in a grubby uniform hung
about with full order, including rifle and kitbag – allowed himself
to be borne along by the noisy, colourful crowd, to the barrier. He
looked lost and terrified, his eyes everywhere. His shoulder-
flashes matched my own.

'Meadows?' I said.

His rifle clattered to the ground. I picked it up. His kitbag
dropped between his boots. He gasped in the heat.

'Are you Meadows?' I said.

'Yes, Sergeant,' he said. He tried to gather together the rifle and
the kitbag, but once again they dropped.

'Take it easy,' I said. 'I'll take the rifle. The jeep's this way. Why
the hell are you wearing boots?'

'I was told to,' he said, as we pressed through beggars. 'Have I
done wrong, Sergeant?'

'Someone's got a strange sense of humour.'

I helped him put his kit in the back of the jeep.

'I'm very thirsty,' he said.

'It's not far. You'll get something there.'

Without his kit he was even thinner. Long bony hands grasping
his knees. I started the engine, used the horn to clear shouting

boot-boys; and joined taxis, camels and carts heading for the bridges of the Nile.

'You're very white,' I said. 'How long have you been in Egypt?'

'A month,' he said. 'I keep out of the sun. I peel easily.'

'What part of Scotland are you from?'

'Aberdeen,' he said. 'Do you know Aberdeen?'

'No.'

He cleared his throat and gave a soft dry cough.

'I miss it. I don't like hot places. Is there a church?'

'A church? In camp, you mean? There's a small chapel . . . just a room.'

'Not in camp. Away from . . . the Army. Is there an English church in Cairo?'

'Yes.'

He relaxed.

'Good.'

'You're religious?'

'Nothing wrong in that, is there?'

'It's . . . unusual, that's all. I don't think I've ever met a religious soldier.'

He sighed.

'Or me, Sergeant.'

*

I signed him in at the Office, and then took him to Barrack room 3. I pointed to the empty bed to the right of the door.

'That's yours,' I said. 'Dump your kit, freshen up, have some lunch, and be back here at one-thirty. We'll go and get your bedding then; and I'll drive you to Headquarters. Okay?'

He pointed to the tins in which the legs of the beds stood.

'What are they for?' he said.

'Things come crawling at night,' I said. 'They climb up the tins, and fall in.' I looked at his white face. 'Didn't you have those in Alex?'

'I was ill for a while,' he said. 'I had a tent, facing the sea. There were lizards. I didn't mind those. You haven't told me your name, Sergeant.'

'Mitchell.'

'And are you in charge . . . of me?'

49

'You'll have your own sergeant at Headquarters. I'm responsible for you here, in this room, and in camp. Have you got a . . . cleaner uniform?'

'There's one in my bag.'

'Get it out, will you?'

He loosened the cord and opened the kitbag. A sour smell arose. He did not seem to notice it.

'I should get those socks washed out today,' I said.

'Yes, Sergeant.'

He held out his cleaner uniform. It was full of creases, and there was a button missing.

'I'll take it to the dhobi-wallahs on my way to the office,' I said. 'They'll press it for you. Collect it after lunch.'

A look of panic came to his face.

'Where is that, Sergeant?'

'I pointed it out to you when we left the office.'

He still looked blank.

'The *tents* . . . ?' I said.

'Oh, yes – the tents. I remember. Thank you, Sergeant.'

'Washrooms are over there: the white brick, see? Next to the lavatories.'

I left him gathering up soap and towel.

Bellah, the young dhobi-wallah, made a face as he inspected Meadows' uniform.

'Very dirty. Who is this?'

'Clean and pressed by one, Bellah. A new man: Meadows.'

'Not camp-style, Sergeant.'

'Just clean it up, Bellah. He'll learn.'

*

Promotion meant being able to eat in the Sergeants' Mess. It was like being made prefect: all the desired privileges. But I was out by one-fifteen.

Bellah called to me.

'He had no money, Sergeant.'

'He won't run away. I'll see him about it.'

Williams was coming out of 3, putting on his cap. He was one of the camp's drivers, but today he was on maintenance: grease-marked fatigues, smell of oil.

'We certainly get them, Sarge, don't we, eh?' He shook his head. 'We certainly do.'

He walked away.

Meadows was hurriedly buttoning his clean uniform.

'That's what I hate about the Army,' he said, looking even more vulnerable without his glasses, his small eyes squinting: 'the lack of privacy.'

His kit was spread on and around the bed, and I groaned at the obvious lack of care. I thought he ought to have some pride: if not in his regiment, at least in himself.

'I bet Alex was glad to get rid of you,' I said. 'Look at the state of these.'

He blinked at the rust-edged mess-tins.

'Perhaps it was the sea . . . '

'It's bloody laziness, that's what it is.'

He put on his glasses.

'Don't start by being angry at me,' he said. 'I thought you might be different . . . '

'I've just taken over this barrack-room, Meadows,' I said. 'The one I had before won every inspection. I can't see it happening here. What did the War Office want with *you*?'

'I could have got out of it, Sergeant,' he said. 'I was down for Theological College. But my father said it would be a fine idea to see something of the world before I entered the Church. He's a Canon.'

'Don't tell anyone else that,' I said. 'Now, let's have a look at you.'

The clean uniform did nothing to change the picture of a man profoundly unsuited to the uncaring precision of military life.

'Put it in some kind or order, will you?' I said, pointing to the kit.

'How?' he said.

'Just . . . pile it up at the top of the bed,' I said slowly.

'Will you help?' he said.

'I don't want to touch anything of it,' I said. I leaned against the corrugated iron of the door, and took out my cigarettes. 'Do you smoke?'

'No,' he said; and *now* there was pride. 'I never have. And I don't drink.'

51

'It's women, then, is it?'

He flushed.

'You're no different from the rest, Sergeant.'

'You have to grow a second skin, Tom,' I said.

'I prefer Thomas.'

'You don't smoke. You don't drink. Your father's a Canon; and you prefer Thomas. You don't make it easy for yourself, do you?'

'Neither did Christ,' he said.

'You've lost me there,' I said.

He put the last of his kit – his small pack – on the bed, and opened it.

'I'd like to put this on the wall,' he said. 'Unless you object . . . '

It was a crucifix, about six inches long: a white ivory Christ on black wood.

'I don't think that's a good idea, Meadows,' I said.

'Neither has anyone else,' he said, resigned.

'Look,' I said: 'you met Williams, yes?'

'Williams?'

'The one who's just left . . . '

'He didn't introduce himself.'

'He'd make your life a misery if you hung that there,' I said.

He looked at me, steadily.

'Since when is Army life not a misery?'

'Okay,' I said. 'You want it up there – you put it up there. And take the consequences.'

'You mean it?'

'Yes.'

'Thank you. Are you a Christian?'

'I'm an atheist.'

'There are no atheists in the front line, Sergeant.'

'What do *you* know about front lines?' I said. 'And don't give me any of that balls. A crucifix is one thing: sermons are another. Don't start evangelising here, right? Now let's go and get your bedding.'

We were tidying-up after a war: paper instead of bullets. An army of pen-pushers. It was a holiday-camp, with discipline.

I left him with Warrant Officer Hedges, and went on to my own department. The afternoon sweltered behind blue blinds, the air sluggish under fans. Soon there would be no afternoon work: the city prostrate.

I had called a meeting of Barrack Room 3 for 1730 hours. I knew all the men by sight. I believed we would get along. Williams had been my only worry. But now there was Meadows.

There was a silence when I entered. Most were waiting to go into the city: they had been paid that morning. There was a smell of Brylcreem. The white cocoons of mosquito-nets were already in place.

'I don't want to keep you,' I said. 'I just wanted to say a few words. You know me. So long as you keep up to the mark, I leave you alone. But I'm not as easy-going as Davies: he knew he was going home, he could relax. I've got another year. I've got a thing about kit: its state tells me about its owner. 8 are a smart lot – but we can be better.'

'With him here?' said Williams, looking at Meadows.

I ignored this.

'And for me,' I said: '*Lights Out* means lights out.' Everyone looked at Williams. The whole camp knew of his stumbling progress at night, his singing; the door crashing back on a darkened barrack room; all lights switched on; the striding duty officer, the running N.C.Os; the Guard room, the final warning . . .

'That's you up the spout, Taff,' said Ridley.

'I don't mind you coming back late,' I said. 'But keep to the rules. Next kit-inspection is Wednesday. I'll run a check on Tuesday night. If you're going to be out – set it up on the bed. Any questions . . . ?'

Wanting to get away, they were silent.

Barrington, an old regular, the Army his only home, happiest in a life where every minute was ordered, said:

'Welcome to 3, Sergeant. That's all.'

I shook his hand. Others came forward, and left. Until only Meadows and the old soldier remained.

'Did W.O. Hedges see about your pay?' I said.

'No,' said Meadows. 'It would have to be Monday, he said.'

'Do you want some money?'

'I don't think so . . . '

I gave him fifty piastres.

'You might want to get something at the canteen. And I should get some blanco from the store. Get started on that equipment this weekend.'

'I would like a hammer and a nail,' he said. 'For my crucifix.'

'Crucifix?' said Barrington.

'And I would like to know where the English church is,' said Meadows. 'Do *you* know?'

Barrington stared at him, as though he were a different species.

'Church?' he said, and slowly shook his head.

*

I was not a drinker, and had no interest in seeing how many pints I could sink before the bar closed. But that night, in the Sergeants' Mess, I put down a few well-watered whiskies as I played Solo. I left before Lights Out, and braced myself for Williams's return.

A radio was playing in 3. A Forces' Network programme – Fats Waller. The crucifix was in place behind Meadows's bed, giving the room a sudden monastic air. Barrington was reading. He opened the mosquito net wider, and looked out.

'Sarge,' he said.

I went over and sat down. Whisky-fumes clouded my brain, and I yawned.

'All alone?' I said.

'You'll have to do something about Meadows.'

'Already?'

'He's a religious maniac. If he gets on to the others as he's got on to me . . . '

'Where is he now?'

'I don't know. I escaped about six; and when I came back he'd gone.' He took a bookmark from the pages, and gave it to me. 'He'd put one of these on every bed.'

The thin card with its yellow silk tassel and border of flowers said: *Wake with Jesus, Walk with Jesus, Sleep with Jesus: Such is Your Salvation.*

'On every bed, has he?' I said, and stood up.

'Don't worry,' said Barrington, 'I've collected them. I've got them here.'

'Good man,' I said, and took them from him. 'Don't tell the others. I'll have a word with him.'

I went out into the dark square framed with lights, crushed the bookmarks into a ball, and threw it into the tall garbage can. Men were drifting back from the city: shapes that crossed and re-crossed yellow windows.

Among them was Williams. Summoning all his control, he tried a salute.

'Good evening, Sergeant.'

'Good evening, Taff,' I said.

He smiled and put a heavy hand on my shoulder.

'Now that's nice, Sarge. All pals together. Merry and bright.'

I followed him into the room.

'Hi there, my lads!' he said.

He steered himself towards his bed.

'Made a special effort tonight, Sarge. Hope you . . . appreciate it.' Then he remembered what he had seen, and turned back. He looked at the crucifix. 'What the hell's that?'

'Leave it, Taff,' I said.

His fingers stayed inches from the cross.

'Little Boy Blue's, is it?' he said. 'Young Mr Meadows. Old Cow-pat. You let him put this up, Sarge?'

'Yes.'

'Then you're bloody mad,' he said, and swung on to his bed.

I went to the door to smoke a last cigarette. Ten minutes before Lights Out, Meadows appeared.

'I found the church, Sergeant,' he said. He sounded very weary. 'It was a long walk. But a beautiful building. I had a word with . . . '

I took him to one side.

'I want one with you,' I said, 'before you go in. I told you – no evangelising.'

'I haven't . . . '

'The bookmarks.'

55

'I thought the men . . . Have they complained?'

'*I'm* complaining. They haven't seen them. I've got rid of them. No more, understand?'

'I suppose so, Sergeant,' he said wearily. 'May I go to bed now?'

'Evening, Padre,' said Williams, as we entered. He was naked, ready to slip between the sheets.

Meadows did not reply. He waited until Lights Out before he began to undress. Later, as men dreamed and spoke in their dreams, and snored and stirred, I sensed a movement from his bed. I sat up.

In the light of a thin moon, Meadows was out of his mosquito-net. He knelt by the side of the bed and said his prayers.

*

I was grateful to Williams, but feared the weekend. But still there was no trouble. He behaved himself. Meadows was solitary: either alone in the pale grass, reading his Bible; or, once again, struggling to get his equipment up to standard. I became less tense, began to enjoy the extra stripe, the position, the better pay.

THREE

On Monday, Warrant Officer Hedges called all his section together in the main office. A thin ramrod of a man, born to wear a uniform, he stood upright against a backdrop of dusty-brown apartment-blocks.

'As you know, I'm going home soon. I'm giving a farewell party in my flat on Friday. You're all invited. Eight until midnight. You'll all come?'

Among the nods and murmurs of agreement, one hand rose.

'Yes, Meadows?' said Hedges.

The frail, bespectacled face lifted.

'I won't be coming, sir.'

'Why not?'

'I . . . ' Meadows shook his head. He cleared his throat, gave that dry nervous cough, and plucked at his collar. 'I don't go to parties, sir.'

There was light laughter among the girls.

'You'll come to this one, Meadows.'

'I'd rather not, sir.'

'It's an order.'

'Oh, is it? Well, then, I suppose . . . '

'So everyone will be there, yes?' said Hedges. 'Good. Thank you.'

As we dispersed, one of the girls – Stella, a dark, ruddy-faced private from Glasgow – took Meadows's arm.

'I don't like parties either, Thomas,' she said. 'I'll look after you. We'll look after each other. Okay?'

'Yes, all right,' he said; but was not comforted.

Driving back to the camp that afternoon, held by traffic at the Seramis Hotel, I saw him walking alone. I sounded my horn, but others were blaring, and he did not lift his head.

The traffic moved, and I pulled alongside.

'Meadows!'

He turned swiftly, defensively.

'Want a lift?'

His shirt was stained with sweat.

'Thank you, Sergeant.'

He sat beside me. The full splendour of the sky showed itself as we crossed the bridge. Crimson clouds coloured the river. A cool breath came off the water and rippled our sleeves.

'I would love this country if it wasn't for the Army,' he said. 'I can understand why holy men chose the desert. I would love to be rich here: to hire a boat and see Luxor.'

'There are tours for servicemen.'

'I mean on my own.'

'How's your kit coming along?'

'Kit? Oh . . . I just have the pouches to do.'

'I'm running a check tomorrow – don't forget.'

'I'll stay in tonight.'

We moved down the first quiet residential road.

'Sergeant?' he said.

'Yes?'

He coughed.

'I'm . . . ' He began again. 'It's Williams.'

'What about him?'

57

'I think he's . . . got it in for me.'

I felt a sudden unexpected anger, born of the way the world was: indifferent to both the strong and the weak.

'Can you blame him?' I said. 'Look at yourself. Have you done that recently? The scruffiest bastard in the camp. Have you seen yourself today? You put a crucifix on the wall, you say your prayers kneeling by your bed; you hide your body like some . . . virgin. What do you expect?'

He turned in his seat and looked at me.

'Some consideration,' he said. 'That's what I expect.'

'Grow a spine,' I said.

'Be a man,' he said: 'yes?'

I was silent.

'You're more angry than Williams,' he said.

*

They were getting ready for supper. Barrington was boxing his kit: trimming cardboard, sharpening the angles.

I crossed to Williams's bed, Meadows following.

'Right, Taff,' I said. 'Where is it?'

I could smell Meadows's sweat.

Williams turned the cigarette-pack in his fingers. The smoke drifted, and he half-closed his eyes.

'Where's what?' he said.

'Meadows's crucifix.'

'Why ask me?'

'Because . . . ' said Meadows.

'Shut it,' I said to him. 'Put it back, Taff, and we'll forget it.'

'What would *I* want with it?' he said. 'Why me? Don't push me, Sarge. Okay? I'm behaving myself, right?'

'Has anyone else seen it?' I said.

'No,' they said.

'Joke over, Taff,' I said. 'Come on.'

'I tell you I haven't touched the bloody thing!'

'Hang on!' called Watson, from behind the partition: 'what's this?'

He came forward, bearing the room's waste-bin. Inside were the fragments of the crucifix: slivers of black and white.

We looked at Meadows; who, in turn, stared at Williams.

'Nothing to do with me, Jock,' said Williams. 'Some of the wogs prefer Allah. Could be anyone.'

'It was you,' said Meadows.

Barrington was moving a finger over the slivers.

'I could mend this for you, Meadows,' he said. 'Give me a couple of days. Good as new. All right?'

Meadows stayed rigid, staring.

I pulled him to his bed.

'Pouches, after supper,' I said.

'Good as new,' said Barrington. 'Don't worry.'

*

On Friday evening I drove Meadows and two other men from the section, across the bridge to Hedges's apartment.

We had survived Wednesday's inspection, in spite of his sub-standard kit. 8 had won again: the old discipline. In 3 the crucifix was back in place: the Christ a little imperfect, hanging a little more uncomfortably. Williams was still keeping his nose clean. A fragile peace prevailed.

A white yacht was moving down the river, breaking the red sun-set water. Music was borne to us, and we heard laughter among the coloured lights. Meadows watched it for a long time, looking back, craning his neck.

Warrant-officers and above had the privilege of living out. Hedges's apartment was on the third floor of a modern block, its living-room windows facing the Nile. There was a smell of warm flesh and perfume and drink and food. The windows were wide, and music played. For some unaccountable reason I thought of beggars in the street below, looking up as the more fortunate feasted.

Hedges, out of uniform, looked like a farmer visiting the city: strange in a lightweight suit, a brown face. He stood behind a range of bottles.

'What'll you have?'

'Whisky,' I said.

He gave me a large glass. I added ice.

'Thomas?' he said.

'That's the first time you've called me that,' said Meadows. 'I suppose it's because you're going home.'

'You're a funny fellow, you know that?' said Hedges. 'Come on, let yourself go.'

'Orange squash, please,' said Meadows.

'You're having a short, my lad,' said Hedges. 'Gin, whisky, vodka . . . you name it. And there's some punch . . . '

'I've never drunk spirits in my life,' said Meadows. 'I didn't want to come – but I'm here. Orange squash, please.'

'Orange squash it is,' said Hedges. 'But I'm disappointed in you, Thomas.'

I walked out on to the balcony. Cairo was spread below, beyond the river. Minarets against the sun's going. Gone. Soon it would grow colder and no one would stand here.

Meadows followed me around for a while, lost while others found themselves in successive glasses. The talk grew louder, there was more laughter, the first drink was spilled. The smoke haze thickened, the music pulsed, other rooms were invaded. Stella, the farmer's daughter, short body held by a red dress showing the start of plump breasts, took Meadows away. He looked back at me, but I did not follow.

People began to sit on the floor. Rimmer had brought his guitar. The old-soldier songs began: *Tipperary . . . Roll me over in the clover . . .* They would get dirtier. I would stay for another fifteen minutes.

*

Something had happened to Meadows. He was one of us. Or them. He found me leaning against the closed windows. His face was burning, his eyes moist, sweat in his hair. He carried a large glass of orange squash. He simpered: that was the only word.

Resting his left hand on my chest, he pushed.

'Hello, Sergeant,' he said.

'Having a good time?'

His tongue felt his lips.

'Better . . . every minute.'

'What are you drinking?'

'Orange.'

I took the glass from him, and sniffed. It was spiked with gin.

'How many of these have you had?'

He tried to count.

'This is . . . does it matter? It's very strong. Stella . . .'

'She ought to know better.'

'Why?'

'It doesn't matter.'

He drank some more.

'Sorry about my kit,' he said. 'I tried, but I couldn't . . .'
He pushed his spectacles on to his forehead. Lifting a vizor, a
carnival mask. A thin, religious boy with fire in his blood. 'It *was*
Williams. The crucifix. He . . . admitted it.'

'It's mended. Forget it.'

'I've met his kind before,' said Meadows. 'There was one at
Dover. He used to . . . ' He closed his eyes.

'Yes?'

'I can't swim, Sergeant.'

'So?'

'He's threatened to . . . ' He finished the glass. 'Would you like
another, Sergeant? I'm going to . . . '

'I shouldn't have any more, Thomas.'

'Why not? It's only orange.'

'It's not.'

'It's not?' He stared into the glass, its orange threads.

'Someone's spiked it with gin. With the best intentions.'

A song ended. Rimmer drank some more lager, wiped his
mouth.

'What next, folks?'

Meadows swung around.

'I know one!' he shouted.

All the faces turned.

'Let's have it, Thomas!' shouted Stella.

He lifted his arms.

'All together now. You know the tune. *Rock of Ages, cleft for
me* . . . '

FOUR

He committed suicide two days later. His body was found in the
sandy butts of a defunct rifle-range at the rear of the camp. He

had shot himself through the mouth: no one knew where he had obtained the one live round. There was no note. A date was fixed for an enquiry; meanwhile, he was to be flown home to wintry Aberdeen, and his parents' incomprehension.

I was ordered to gather together his personal effects.

The tough cardboard box stamped *WD* rested on the end of his bed. I was alone in 3, folding a towel over his shaving-kit. It was early afternoon, Monday.

A shadow crossed the bed. It was Williams.

On the night of the party, he had returned from his own drinking in Cairo, slammed back the door, hitting the bed where Meadows, his third bout of vomiting over, was settling to sleep; had switched on all the lights, rocked Meadows's shoulder through the mosquito-net, and shouted: *Want to buy a battle-ship, Jock?* As I got out of bed, he had straightened. *Okay, Sarge, okay. Lights out. I'm for my pit. 'Night, all. 'Night, Jock.*

Now he stood in the doorway, watching.

'Okay if I come in?' he said.

'Do what you like.'

He stayed near me.

'Take what you came for, and go,' I said. 'You *have* got work to do, haven't you?'

'I came to see you, Sarge.'

I put the folded towel in the box.

'Why'd he do it?' he said.

I said nothing.

'Trouble was: he couldn't take a joke,' said Williams.

I felt if I spoke, I would rage. So stayed silent.

'I . . . I wanted to know . . . '

'Yes?' I said, and looked up. He appeared uncertain, mixed emotions in his face.

'I wanted to know if I could have that,' he said.

'What?'

He pointed to the crucifix, still on the wall.

'That.'

'What the hell for?'

He struggled for the words, hands moving as if to pluck them from the air.

'I'd just . . . like to have it, Sarge. Please.'

'His parents . . . '

'I could write to them. Explain . . . '

'And what would you say?' Diary, pens, writing-paper in my hands, I looked at him. 'How you hounded him, made his life a misery? Say that, would you?'

'Me?' He was frankly astonished. 'I was just . . . playing around. Like we all do. Like others do to me. I . . . '

'He said you threatened him.'

'*Me?*' He shook his head. 'I admit I'm a bit of a bastard when I've had a few, but I'm okay otherwise. Look, I'll lay off the booze if I can have it, right?'

'Take it,' I said.

It was as if I had granted him absolution. His face cleared.

'You mean it?'

'Until the next pint.'

He lifted the cross from the wall, then worked the nail free. Fine dust fell.

'Thanks, Sarge,' he said. 'I appreciate it.'

'What are you going to do with it?'

He looked at me as though I were a child.

'Put it on *my* wall, what else?'

'Until the next pint.'

He smiled.

'I may surprise you,' he said.

*

They had not sung *Rock of Ages*. They had laughed at him loud and long, and wiped tears from their eyes. *I don't believe it! What did he say? Rock of Ages? You're priceless, you know that, Thomas?*

The gin burning his blood, he stood there, betrayed; then dropped his glass and ran from the apartment. He spoke to no one after that night. And on Sunday, took his rifle to the range . . .

The inquiry was held, and its members said *Suicide*. The CO and Captain Leicester wrote careful letters to his parents. A new man from Ismalia moved into his bed. *Rock of Ages* was what people remembered, smiling. Years hence, in smoky bars and quiet kitchens and at the end of Rotary Club lunches, men would

say: *We had one once, chap called Meadows, in Cairo, in '45.
He . . .*

*

The crucifix stayed above Williams's bed. He drank only Coke,
sitting alone in the canteen.

He was within a week of going home.

He began to complain about his eyes. He came back from
Cairo wearing a pair of large rimless spectacles.

His walk changed: once easy, oiled, purposeful – he was
slower, and his head inclined to the right, as though he listened to
an unseen companion.

On Tuesday I looked at his kit.

'What do you call this?' I said.

The glasses made him studious, thinned his face. He touched
the large pack with one finger.

'What, Sergeant?' he said.

'Look at it,' I said. 'You're not saying that's finished, are you?'

'I . . . I thought it was.' He seemed drained of strength.

'It's your last inspection,' I said. 'For Christ's sake, make *some*
effort.'

He twitched, and one hand touched his cheek.

'I don't think you ought to curse, Sergeant,' he said. He tipped
his head to one side, listening. He nodded. 'Jesus has no place
here.'

Someone laughed. But the others were motionless, watching
us.

'Come outside,' I said.

'Why?'

'I want to talk to you.'

'May I bring my book?' he said.

'Jesus!' said Watson.

Some of the old fire, the old power, returned.

'I'm warning you,' said Williams: 'watch your mouth!'

He searched among his spread, sagging kit, and brought out
the book.

'Let's go, Sergeant,' he said.

Once outside, he ducked under the weight of the sun.

'I . . . I don't want to go near the swimming-pool,' he said.

64

'I wasn't intending to.'

Relieved, he said: 'Anywhere shady.'

The canteen was closed, but I pulled rank and got two Cokes. Behind the green-painted prefabricated building was a patch of boot-beaten earth margined by whitewashed stones. There were wooden tables and chairs under dusty palms, and a few bleached umbrellas. I joined him there. He closed the book, marking the place. I took it from him. *The Purposes of God.*

'Where did you get this?' I said.

'I bought it at the English Church. There's a bookstall.'

'It's got Meadows's name in it.'

'Has it?' he said. He glanced at the flyleaf. 'So it has.'

We drank the warm Coke.

'I hate flies,' he said. 'Why do you think God made flies?'

'And where did you get the bookmark?' I said, smoothing the silk tassel.

There was a battle in his face. And Williams won. He surfaced.

'You've got to help me, Sarge,' he said. 'He's everywhere I bloody look.' Distracted, he beat a fly from his lips. 'He keeps . . .'

And floundered.

'Guilt, is it?' I said.

He calmed. Even managed a grin.

'What have I got to be guilty about?'

'Take the crucifix off the wall,' I said.

He literally shook.

'I . . . I can't do that.'

'Take it off and get rid of it. Get rid of everything that's his. You're free in four days. Where have you got all this stuff *from*?'

'That's the trouble,' he said. He wiped sweat off his face. 'I don't know.'

'Report sick,' I said. 'Tomorrow.'

'Then they'd have me, wouldn't they?' he said. 'No, I'll stick it out.' Then he lost the battle. The eyes narrowed behind the lenses. 'May I have my book back, Sergeant? I don't want any more Coke. It's too hot here. I shall be home soon. Out of it.'

*

After breakfast the next morning I went back to 3. The empty room was beautifully correct: we had helped him with his kit. Once back in Wales, among green rain-washed mountains, with his own people . . .

Inspection was at nine-thirty. I had forty-five minutes.

I went through his locker. There were a number of religious books, all new, all bearing Meadows's angular signature. I found ten or so bookmarks, with differing silks and texts. There was a small framed photograph of an elderly couple, standing either side of their son, behind them the open door of a grey-stone church.

I gathered all these together, and pulled the crucifix from the wall. It broke in my hands. I put everything into a large envelope, took it to the incinerator behind the cookhouse, and watched it burn.

When I returned at the end of the day, driving the jeep through the entrance, he flagged me down near the guardroom and climbed in. He looked weary, but triumphant, and the spectacles had gone.

'Thanks, Sarge,' he said. 'I was . . . bloody terrified.'

Late on Friday night, Captain Leicester came into the Sergeants' Mess to say goodbye. Slightly tipsy from the evening's celebrations, he bought drinks all round.

'Good luck, sir,' we said, raising our glasses.

'Sorry to be going, really,' he said. 'Home posting. The wilds of Wiltshire. Ah, well.'

And I thought of the woman he was leaving behind. Imprint of sunblinds on a body; and the winds of March roaring across Salisbury Plain.

'Just come from the canteen,' he said. 'A few thick heads tomorrow.'

'Was Williams there?' I said.

'Very much so,' said Leicester. 'In good voice. Making up for lost time.'

'Good,' I said.

FIVE

Saturday morning at nine. The truck was waiting for Port Said. Williams, pale and hung-over, shook the last hand, and reached for his kit.

66

I picked up his rifle and small pack.

'Thank you,' he said. He looked around the room: the military life, softened by personal possessions. 'I won't be sorry to leave this. Goodbye, lads.'

We stepped out into the square. I thought: *This will happen to me, in a year's time.* And the future opened like a hole.

'What will you do, Taff?' I said.

Alone now, crossing the sand-grained asphalt, he looked at me.

'I'm going home to think, Sergeant.'

'No plans, then?' I said, keeping my voice level.

'Many,' he said. 'But not for the authorities to know.'

And yet here was Williams's body walking under early morning sunlight, and signs gave directions and arrows pointed.

We were the last to arrive at the truck. Captain Leicester, sharp and glittering in his best uniform, made a tick on his paper.

'Come on, Williams: get a move on.'

Happy faces looked down, hands reached. He climbed up, awkwardly.

Leicester returned my salute and went to join the driver.

I gave Williams his rifle and small pack. They clattered to the floor. He shifted closer on the seat and looked down.

'Just a moment, Sergeant,' he said.

He took the spectacles from his shirt pocket, and put them on. He took a pen and a bookmark from the same pocket, and wrote something on the back of the card. He gave the familiar nervous cough, and cleared his throat.

'I'd like you to have this, Sergeant,' he said. 'If you're ever in my part of the country . . . '

The tassel was green. The printed words said: *Not a sparrow falls . . .* I turned the card over. He had written an address. *24 Lough road, Aberdeen, Scotland.*

Leicester leaned out of the cab.

'All fit, Sergeant?'

I slammed my hand against the side of the truck.

'Take it away, driver!'

Wheels turned. The men cheered. The truck took the incline. Dust began to drift over the camp, towards open iron doors.

The Second Mrs Day

Burying her mother, she lifted her head and saw, past the wind-tugged surplice of the priest, a white pick-up disturbing the dust on the slip road; and when it stopped, light shot from its windshield, blinding her.

He came two days later, wearing a tidy suit. She appreciated that: his thought. By that time the silence had got to her. Many times she had wished her mother dead – an end to both their pain. Now that the querulous voice had stopped, there was nothing to do.

She saw him through the screen door: the kerosene man, the two-week delivery. Always a Wednesday, in the morning, and coffee. Today was Friday, in the afternoon.

He settled his shoulders, paused, and nodded. Then tapped.

He always looked defensive – as if about to be attacked. A half-raised arm to protect himself. A constant wariness, born of what hurt? He tried to take care of himself, but it was not enough. The suit was tidy – worn perhaps twice a year – but the man was not. Some said he dyed his hair: its blackness sat strange above a life-battered face. His moustache was thickening from grey to white, and his eyes were pale and brown and moist, like a stream-bed. The cloth of the suit was creased with hanging, not wearing; and the collar of his shirt was buckled.

'Helen,' he said.

Over coffee, he talked about his own dead wife.

'When they're gone, you know you never did enough,' he said.

'I did more than enough.'

'That's true.'

'What can I do for you, Mr Day?'

'Walter,' he said. He waited. Then said: 'You don't want to stay out here alone. You have any money?'

'We were on relief. You know that.'

He looked around the room. An old woman's room.

'I need some help', he said. 'And some . . . feminine company. Neville's not suited. He should be in Fairfax -- at the plant. I've told him to go.'

Helen Baur was thirty-three, unmarried, a virgin, all her beauty in her large direct eyes, her body thin and white, her hands ringless.

Warily he searched for words that would give no offence. He had admired her for a long time: her quiet strength, her constancy. Chained to an old witch.

'I'm sixty, Helen,' he said.

'So?'

'Beginnin' to feel it, too.' He shifted his shoulders. 'Ache in the mornin's. Fall asleep soon as we close.'

'Would you teach me to drive?'

'That what you want?'

'I'm not begging.'

'If that's what you want — to drive. Sure I'll teach you.'

'A housekeeper, right?' she said.

'An' some help. When I ain't around.'

'Nothing else?'

'No. I guess not. It'd have to be Walter.'

'Walter.'

'You'd take the talk?'

'You mean there are small minds in Pearl?'

He took out a tin and began to roll a cigarette. Work was grained into his hands: all lines drawn as if with a pen.

'When can you come?' he said.

Now she looked around the room, and there was nothing that held her.

'Now,' she said.

'Say an hour or two? Get things together?

'I mean *now*. Right now. Taking nothing, starting fresh. You understand that?'

'I guess so. We'd have to come back sometime . . . '

'You could fix some kind of sale,' she said. She moved swiftly from her chair, as swiftly as he had moved, once. 'Not even a comb. Yes?'

He caught something of her excitement. He put the made cigarette, unlit, back in the tin.

70

'Okay, Helen,' he said. 'Let's go.'

*

Neville watched the lizard, stone at the ready. It skittered a few inches nearer: spring green against the dust. Preparing to throw, the chair grated under him, and the lizard whipped away between the pumps. Neville threw the stone anyway: the tin sign clanged.

Day's Store and Station, six miles east of Pearl, Arizona, forty miles west of Fairfax.

She saw it coming out of the heat-haze: white clapboard against the mountain – a better home than her own. A staging-post, before what . . . ?

'I'm grateful, Mr Day,' she said. 'Walter.'

'Time you lived a little,' he said. 'I always thought . . . '

'Yes?'

'It don't matter. Maybe later . . . '

Neville saw the pick-up; and then the woman behind the hazy windshield. And freedom tugged at him like a hand. He got off the chair, out of the shade, and went to his motorcycle. He wheeled it into the sun. Walter Day got out of the pick-up.

'Hi, Miss Baur,' said Neville.

'I'll pay you the full week,' said Walter. He took the bills from his pocket. 'No hard feelin's.'

'No,' said Neville. 'Maybe you're right.'

'I am,' said Walter. 'You get to that plant. They can always call me here: I'll tell a few lies for you.'

'Thanks, Mr Day,' said Neville. The wind stirred his yellow hair. 'Guess I'll go. Watch the end pump, Miss Baur: got a kick like a mule.'

'She ain't tendin' no pumps,' said Walter. 'Least, not permanent. She looks after the store.'

'Yes, sir,' said Neville.

The bike roared beneath him. Grains stung their faces. The lizard shook its head and tried for the dry grass.

*

People came out from Pearl for a week or so, buying unneeded gas or cereals or fruit or kerosene: just to see. Some imagined sex in that solitude; others, more realistic, saw it simply as a solution:

thin dutiful daughter and lonely widower – it might work. Helen Baur, the quiet one; Walter Day, the deserving. Colourless, they were left alone.

One day six weeks later, Neville's mother, driving by, called in with the news of her son. Walter was filling the tank of a big *Marlboro* truck; the driver stretching his arms to the sun. Mrs Richmond glimpsed a movement out back, and found Helen in a tinted greenhouse.

Flowers and plants were thriving under glass and sprinklers. Mrs Richmond wiped the base of her throat.

'This is nice,' she said. 'The woman's touch.'

She chose a flowering cactus: a rich pink spreading from dry lizard-like fronds.

'And what is *that*?' she said, pointing to the left through the glass. Outside, the air was only slightly cooler. High white clouds in a burning sky.

The metal of the new blue coupé was too hot to touch. The leather-smell, the sky-reflecting chrome, the hood pointing to the mountain.

'It's Walter's,' said Helen.

'It's beautiful,' said Mrs Richmond. 'And expensive. Not the car he'd choose, honey.'

'I got my licence last week,' said Helen.

'*A-ha*!' said Mrs Richmond, and winked.

The truck's air-brakes gasped, its engine roared; and Walter joined them. Mrs Richmond saw that he looked trimmer, chipper – more cared-for.

'Admiring the car,' she said.

'It's Helen's,' said Walter. 'She just got her licence.'

Helen looked away.

'It's yours, Walter. You paid the cash.'

'*Ours*, then,' he said. 'Don't argue, girl.'

'I'd like a foreign car,' said Mrs Richmond. 'But Steve, he . . .' She sighed. 'Well, I guess I'd better make a move. I had a letter from Neville, Walter. He wishes to be remembered. Doing okay, enjoying himself.'

'Better he shoulda gone to the plant,' he said. 'What's with the Marines . . . ?'

'He'll see the world,' said Mrs Richmond.

'No place like home,' said Walter. 'Right, Helen?'

She smiled, but did not answer.

*

A few days on, around seven in the evening, the earth cooling, a pine-scented wind bearing the night down from the mountain, they sat in canvas chairs at the rear of the store. Walter burped quietly.

'You make a good stew, Helen,' he said. 'Jesus, I'm tired.' He closed his eyes, his fingers linked over his stomach.

A bird sang reedily in a bush. And stopped. The only sound was the wind combing the grasses. The collar of Helen's shirt lifted and fell, like a wing.

Her right hand moved back and forth on the wooden arm of the chair. Her fingers tapped, and were still. A car came down the road, going fast, and began to climb the mountain. She listened to it, until the sound was the faintest mark on the air. Gone. The bird gave voice to a single note, and left the bush.

She turned her head and looked at Walter. His eyes open, he had been watching her. She gave a half-smile. He pushed himself out of the chair and went into the house. She leaned back against the canvas strap and looked up at the sky. It was the tenderest mauve, spread with puffs of orange cloud which, even as she watched, began to deepen.

He came out of the house. He was holding an envelope. Without speaking, he gave it to her.

'What is it?' she said, and then saw what was written. *Helen's Escape Money.*

'Open it,' he said.

Inside was a thousand dollars, in crisp hundreds.

'I don't understand,' she said.

He pulled his chair closer to hers, and sat down. The blue of his shirt echoed the shadows on the mountain. She could smell the heat of his body.

'You notice how your head goes up when you hear a car?' he said. 'You notice how you talk to people: asking where they're from, where they're going? I don't think I've ever met such a restless character as you, Helen. You've been nowhere, you've done nothin'. You're free, and you're feelin' it, right?'

'Escape money?' she said.

'I want you to take the car an' go,' he said. 'Go anywhere you like. Spend the thousand.'

'You've done enough already, Walter,' she said. 'Here.'

'I don't want it, Helen. I've been careful, but money can go dead in a bank. It's for spendin'. I've got my health and strength – you can't buy that.'

Impulsively, she touched his hand. It was their first contact, and she did not know what havoc she caused.

'Come with me,' she said. 'We'll take two weeks . . . '

'No,' he said. 'I never wanted to go anywhere but here. Me and the mountain. Get your things, and go. We'll be here when you get back.'

'Supposing I don't come back?'

'I thought of that. I'll take the risk. Just send a card; call me sometime.'

'I'll go in the morning.'

'You'll go now,' he said. 'Before you find reasons. You want to go, don't you?'

And the distance opened like a book, or a map, or a door.

*

Her fine gold hair had been pulled back by a thin black ribbon. Now, driving the car with one hand, she released it. Air blustered it about her face, then it streamed. She let the ribbon go and it swirled away from her fingers. She put her hand back on the wheel.

Pearl came out of the red dusk with its neoned Main Street, its pool hall, its bar, its drugstore. Then it was gone, and she said goodbye with a long blast of the horn.

She had no plans. She would go where fancy led. All she knew was that she would never return. She switched on the radio, and the bouncy country-and-western banjos matched her own animation. She felt joined to the car's efficiency, that smooth mesh of oil and metal: together, preceded by powerful headlamps, they raced towards the future, the glittering potential.

Soon she drove through a dark land, pockmarked by the lights of distant ranches; dazzled at intervals by other cars sighing back into the past.

Gone midnight, south of Havasu Lake, close to the border,

74

brighter neon dulled the stars: *Wayfarer Inn*. She liked the name.

A small fountain bubbled in the foyer, water spilling from the mouth of a blue ceramic fish. Voices were raised in the room beyond the desk.

' . . . too damned smart. If he worked as hard at what I'm paying him for, he . . . '

Helen rang the bell.

A small neat man came from the room, changing his expression from irritation to welcome.

Within an hour she was still awake, lying straight in clean sheets, eyes open to the shadowed room, listening to a Phoenix DJ: *Hallo out there, all you night-owls . . .*

*

At first the newness disturbed her: daylight sharper on functional furniture, drapes, Navajo patterns. But only for seconds. Then she remembered, and stretched her suddenly unfamiliar hands and arms above her head. She turned in the pillows and looked at the window. Water was reflected: it rippled on the ceiling. She had fallen asleep to Damone: now another DJ played Jim Reeves.

The door opened.

A tall young man in white shirt, blue bow-tie, blue slacks and white sneakers came in, carrying a tray.

'Good morning, Miss Baur.'

She drew the sheet around her, remembering she had ordered breakfast in bed: the first of many intended indulgences.

'Good morning.'

He leaned across her and clipped the tray to the bed. His face was brown and narrow, his thick hair bleached yellow-white, and he was proud of his teeth – the smile continued.

'I'm Ty Weller,' he said. 'Your breakfast, ma'am.'

Magician-like, he whipped away the cloth, and she smelled coffee and toast and pancake and bacon. A miniature pack of cereals rested in a blue bowl.

'Thank you,' she said.

He moved lightly and silently to the window and opened the drapes. Sunlight woke in every polished surface. A wider expanse of water glittered on the ceiling.

'Great car: your Merc,' he said, without turning around.

'Yes.'

'Staying long or passing through?'

'Passing through. What is the water?'

'Swimming-pool, Miss Baur.'

Even as he spoke, they heard a splash.

'Mr Scott, dead on time,' said Ty. He stood, looking out. Light lit his shirt, showed the lines of his body. He stepped away from the window and looked at her.

'*Bon appetit*,' he said; smiled, and left.

*

Showered and dressed, she looked down at the pool, its floor a mosaic of intertwined dolphins. Beyond it, watched over by a growing sun, was the border and California. She went to the bed and folded her nightdress.

Something had once again angered the small neat man at the desk. He used the *Paid* stamp with some force, and counted change from the hundred with swift, clipped numbers.

'Stay longer next time, Miss Baur,' he said, but it was automatic, without warmth, and he acknowledged the coldness. 'Excuse me: problems with the help. Have a safe journey.'

'Thank you,' she said.

She felt as fresh as the air. Problems were for others. She patted the car as though it were an animal: faithful, ready to serve.

She drove out on to the highway. Ahead was the white-wood bridge spanning the Colorado river. He was standing in the grass, a brown bag looped over his left shoulder, his right hand raised.

She stopped. All around them was movement; the sun-ovalled slide of the river, the bending of thin trees and grasses, the passing of cars and trucks, the swooping of small birds.

He put his hand on the door.

'Am I in luck?' he said.

'I think so.'

He got in.

'Where are you making for?' she said.

'Anywhere but here.'

She waited for a bus to pass, then pulled out.

'Are you the help that's causing problems?' she said.

'You hear about that?'

'In passing.'

He had discarded the bow-tie, his shirt open at the throat. Sleeves pushed back, the fine hairs of his arms shone. Both Helen and he were conscious of a heightened physical presence: he, because it was normal, functioning whenever a woman was found, a warm awakening, a reflex; she, feeling it in her throat, closing on a breath, drying her mouth.

'I'm glad to get the hell out,' he said. 'I'm not the type.'

She cleared her throat.

'What would you like to do?'

'Drive forever in a Mercedes,' he said. 'This is my kind of car. You driving somewhere special?'

Some innate caution warned her to be careful: but that was the voice of the careful past, and she ignored it.

'No,' she said.

He put his arm across the back of the seat.

'You mean: you're just . . . '

'Just driving.'

'Hey, great!' he said. 'You know California?'

'No.'

'Maybe I could show you around.'

'Haven't you got a home?'

'No. And I like it that way. You married?'

'No. And I'm thirty-three.'

'What the hell does age matter?' he said. 'You want me to get out?'

'No,' she said.

*

It was he who suggested the picnic. They stopped at a roadside store to buy food. The interior with its signs and smells made her think of Walter, but Arizona was another state.

'And some wine?' said Ty.

'Why not?' she said.

They bought two carafes of red, and he carried the box to the car.

'Okay if I drive?' he said.

'Sure, go ahead.'

And she was content to watch him; and then the land.

77

The back road led to a glint of water. Here a stream ran and wildfowl called. Not a human in sight, but an airliner shone silver, and faded. They left the car in the shade of trees, and unpacked the box at the stream's edge. They ate the cheese salad, the hardboiled eggs, the tomatoes, and drank wine from paper cups. They lay in the grass, and unseen insects ticked away the seconds.

His flesh burned under her hands. He was expert: her lips, breasts, the insides of her thighs. She was ready long before he entered her. The air was a hot confusion of leaves and sunrays, teeth at her nipples, gasps at her ear. And then her shout.

He moved off her.

She tamed her breathing, and slept.

The noise of the car's engine woke her. She lifted her head from warm grass. Ty was at the wheel, and the car was reversing. She watched it idly. Then . . . knew.

Naked, she ran. The Mercedes straightened. She reached it as the engine roared. She held on to the door. He turned and hit her full in the mouth.

Flat on her back, blood beginning to trickle down her throat, she heard the car crash through bushes, and away.

*

She sat near the front window of the Sheriff's office, beside her empty coffee cups. Police officers who had at first been sympathetic and concerned, now left her alone. Rape they understood. She had said simply: *We made love*. No longer angered by their glances and the occasional laugh, she moved her tongue on her swollen lips, and felt the sun, made more powerful by the glass, inch up her arm. Outside, other women shopped, held the hands of children, talked with friends.

The least derisive of the officers came by again.

'No news,' he said. 'More coffee?'

It was painful to speak. Two of her teeth were loose.

'No, thank you,' she said.

And then she saw the white pick-up, coming slowly from the right.

'He's here,' she said. Standing up, she swayed.

'Take it easy,' said the officer.

'I'm all right.'

Light flashed as the suncaught outer door opened. Walter came in, and the unknown town became home. His face reflected her own hurt. He moved towards her.

'Hold it, sir,' said the young know-it-all officer, he who had laughed.

'I've come for Miss Baur,' said Walter.

'Miss Baur's been a bad girl,' said the young officer.

'When I want your opinion, smart-ass, I'll ask for it,' said Walter. He pushed past the officer and took Helen's arm. 'You okay?'

Withheld tears came, sharp and hot.

'I'm sorry, Walter,' she said.

'It doesn't matter. We'll go home now.'

'Just leave your name, address and phone-number, sir,' said the young officer.

'We have those, Rayner,' said the other officer. 'Smarten up. We'll be in touch, ma'am.'

'Catch the bastard, you hear?' said Walter. 'Or I will.'

'Yes sir, Mr Day,' said the young officer.

Helen blinked in hot sunlight, the headache hammering. Her hand fluttered to her face. Walter saw her seated safely in the pick-up, and went away. He came back with ice wrapped in a piece of cloth. She held it to her forehead as he swung the pick-up for the border.

Soon the ice was water. She wrung the cloth out of the window.

'Better?' he said.

'Some,' she said. 'I . . . '

'You don't have to tell me.'

'But the car . . . '

'It'll turn up, Helen. We all have to learn.'

'He took everything: the car, all the money . . . '

'Who'd have thought otherwise?' said Walter. 'It's the way the world's made. You're surprised? You nursed your mother too long – an' that's the truth.'

*

A month later, Ty still free, the car unfound, she told Walter she was pregnant.

79

He manoeuvered a small bone to his lips, and put it on the edge of his plate.

'You want to get rid of it?' he said.

'No.'

They were married in a quiet, flowered room in Phoenix; spent the night of their honeymoon in a motel-room lit by the lances of passing trucks; his lovemaking a kind of unspoken gratitude. Returning through Fairfax, they put an announcement in the *Courier*.

People from Pearl, noticing Helen grow, counted on their fingers, smiled, and spoke of shot-guns.

The boy, Glenville Mark Day, was born on Monday the 3rd March, at 4 pm.

She was holding him for the first time, in a bed facing the door, when Walter came visiting. He stood there, his arms full of flowers.

And then fell among crushed stalks and flying petals.

*

Once he had said: *I don't like the idea of being underground.*

And so she had scattered his ashes on the mountain. On the anniversaries of his death, she climbed between trees dusted with late snow or warm with the first sun of the year, and stayed silent, looking down at the new store his money had built, the men she employed at the pumps and in the workshops.

Ty's file grew dust in the Sheriff's office, and the car was lost forever.

In the fifth year of Walter's death and Glenville's birth, alone in the store, the sun casting a welcome shadow across fly-patrolled glass, she heard the pump-bell ring, and looked up.

A large corn-yellow bus, hung about with streamers and balloons, came to a stop. On its side the green words said: *Craven Home for Paraplegics, La Junta, Colorado*. She watched as Clark went to the driver.

The door of the bus slid back, and a girl appeared. She came in to the store. She was baby-faced, in Aliceband and jeans, and on her T-shirt was printed *Craven All-Stars*.

'We're bone-dry out there,' she said. 'Guess it'll be five six-packs of Coke. You have any lager? One six of lager. And straws. And one each of those sandwiches.'

She plucked at her shirt as Helen lifted the cans from the freezer.

'It's a hot one,' she said.

'Going to a game?' said Helen.

'Game?'

'*All-Stars*,' said Helen.

'No, not this time. Just taking a few guys to the coast.'

Helen helped her carry the drink and the food to the bus. Clark clipped shut the tank-cover as the driver came back from the toilet.

It was hot inside the bus. Hot with more than heat, or perhaps she imagined it. There was a faint smell of urine. Ranged down either side, anchored to the floor, were men in wheelchairs: young and old men, but mostly young. Most of them wore comic paper hats, and had streamers draped over their shoulders. There was a kind of gaiety; false or not, she did not know.

'Beer, not Coke!' they cried.

'Beer at the beach,' said the girl: 'I know you guys.' She looked at Helen. 'You want to help some more?'

Helen chose the line to the right. Most of the men had lifeless arms and hands. Small trays swung out from the side of the bus. Helen put the Coke on the trays, opened the cans, and bent straws to eager lips. The men said *Thank you*, and nodded. Some were goodlooking, and she thought of the waste. Or the triumph. Yes.

She reached the last man. He appeared the most severely disabled: held in an airy cage of white steel.

It was Ty Weller.

They looked at each other. He, above his dead body, saw a woman he had forgotten. She, a man she could never forget. His head was locked in a metal collar, so highly-polished that she could see her distorted reflection.

'Coke?' she said.

He could do nothing: neither speak nor move. She opened the can, put in the straw, bent it, and held it to his lips. He drank deeply, then his eyes signalled that she should stop: as though the icy liquid pained. She took the can away.

The girl reached her.

'Okay, Ty?' she said. 'You want to eat?'

He blinked, twice.

'Maybe later?' she said.

He blinked once.

'Thank you,' the girl said to Helen. 'Guess we'd best be making a move.'

Helen looked at Ty. He tried to frame words, his lips aching above his fixed jaw. He closed his eyes.

The driver was waiting below the steps. He touched the peak of his gaudy jockey-cap, and helped her down. Then he entered, and closed the door.

She stood before the pumps and watched the bus move by. Ty appeared, vainly trying to turn his head. She had seen eyes like that in terrified cattle. Then he was gone.

*

When she could see the bus no longer, she went back into the store and stood in front of the wall-telephone.

She stood there some time.

Then it was time to collect her son from school.

RELATIONS

ONE

Out of the Sunday city with its marvels, they sped west. His father, free of the office for a week, wore a new panama with a floral band. His mother, everything out of her hands at last, began to fall asleep in the back.

Steven Slatterley, sixteen, fumed.

Green was the colour of boredom. Of trees and grass and parks; rainsoaked deckchairs and swings.

He loved the city. He would have preferred it walled: everything contained, manmade and sleek, the colours metallic, not a tree in sight. A neon heaven, with everything for sale.

He hated the country: the bare hills that never changed, the throat-catching farm smells, the silence, the stupid sheep with their strange polished eyes and sudden panics; the empty villages where only water moved.

'This is the last time, Dad,' he said.

'Yes.'

'I mean it.'

'So you said.'

'I could be with Max now. He . . . '

'Could we leave it, *please*?' said his mother, without opening her eyes. 'I really think I have had enough. Hour after hour . . . '

'I don't know why I *have* to come.'

Still with her eyes closed, she said:

'Because they love to see you. One week a year – it's not a lot to ask. Other boys would love a week on a farm . . . '

'I'm not other boys. I'm me. And this is the last time.'

*

Early evening now, the last town an hour behind them, they

climbed the hills, heading into the Black Mountains. It was dark enough for headlamps where the road parted a wood. A fox was lit, its eyes a white burning.

Once free of the trees, up there on bald earth, they could see the farm warmed by the sun's going: a cubed pink against blue shoulders.

'Isn't that a sight?' said his mother. 'Now, Steven, isn't that something?'

His left arm resting on the open window, he could smell night coming out of the grounds: that damp breath – and did not answer.

'How could anyone *not* like coming here?' she said. 'Wouldn't you like to retire here, Joe?'

'A week's enough,' said her husband.

She breathed in the quiet.

'It's the peace,' she said.

They took the old track to the farm. Soon the dogs came racing: black and white bolts of energy, lolling tongues, hysterical barking, keeping pace.

'Hallo, Dan!' she said, waving. 'Hallo, Emma!'

A figure stood beyond the open gate. Behind her the farm grew lights. The dogs bounded and bounced, until silenced to a swift beating of tails. His grandmother was thinner than he remembered, but he had not forgotten her smell: that combination of clean, starched linen, and flesh that housed the sun. She was darker against the night, and her hands were cold.

'Why, you're taller than ever,' she said, as though it were a marvel. 'You're taller than your dad.'

'Where's Pop?' he said.

'In the house. Just got in. You know him: won't stir himself unless he has to. How are you, Joe? Smart hat, that is.'

She kissed her daughter, and Steven and his father carried the suitcases into the house.

Pop was fixing his hearing-aid: sharp whistles that sent the dogs hiding under tables. He was a small, balding man, becoming fixed with the years: hills becoming mountains; mountains part of the sky. Shy, he sought refuge in ancient jokes and monologues: not imaginative enough to know he bored. Now, faced with a week's disturbance, he acted a kind of pleasure.

The dogs came out from under the tables and joined in – until they were bundled out.

His grandfather's hands were hard as wood, knotted with old blisters.

'Same room?' said Steven.

'Yes,' said his grandmother. 'I can't get over how tall . . . '

Others would have appreciated the view. The strong dark mountains, a far field lit by the last angle of the sun, the cluster of clouds at the horizon, the mat of sheep, darkening. But to Steven, it had the bone-aching quality of *sameness*: it was as if he had never gone away. Once a year since he was two: fourteen visits. Only he had grown.

He began to unpack.

*

Supper over, they sat around a fire framed by logs drying on the hearth. Other logs, burning, spat sparks towards the watchful dogs. Steven's mother was trying to keep awake, her head falling forward, recovering.

'Got a surprise for you, Steven,' said his grandmother.

'Oh?' he said.

'Some new people have taken over the old Evans' place,' she said. 'Not Welsh, mind, but nice. They have a boy your age: Colum. He's on half-term, too. You can go around together. I've asked him to call in tomorrow morning. He's finding it a bit lonely, up there.'

His mother opened her eyes.

'Well, some company for you,' she said.

'Yes.'

'I've cleaned and oiled the old bike,' said Pop. 'Still going strong. Get you as far as Brecon, easy.'

'Thanks,' he said.

'You'll break your neck in a minute, Mary,' said his father, as sleep once more weighted her head. He yawned. 'Never fails, does it: the different air?' He stood up. 'Let's go.'

'Pop, you ready?' said Steven's grandmother. She tutted. 'Switched off again. *Pop!*' She looked at Steven. 'You can stay and watch TV, if you like.'

Alone in the living-room, he watched Clint Eastwood rob a bank.

As he climbed the stairs to bed, he heard an owl cry, close to the house.

TWO

He was woken by a thin scratch of sound: a cock crowing into pre-dawn mist. He turned in the bed and slept again until his grandmother brought him a mug of tea.

'Did you hear the owl last night?' she said.

The tea was strong and foreign.

'Yes.'

'I wondered if you did. Remember how you cried, that first time, when you were young? When the owl . . . '

'No.' he said.

'Of course you do,' she said. 'You went running along the landing for your mother, but came in our bedroom by mistake. You remember. I'll never forget your face.'

She laughed.

'I don't remember that,' he said.

'Well, you were young. It was a long time ago.' She moved out of the shaft of sunlight. 'It's a beautiful morning.'

Cleaning his teeth in a different bathroom, the half-open window showing a narrow column of green and blue, the day stretched like a year. Backed by mermaid tiles, his face was equally alien, fit only for the city.

The doors of the house were wide open, as though the air visited. Pop was already out on the hill. Steven's parents slept on, drugged by silence. The breakfast was huge, and he ate everything.

'Sharpens you up: fresh air,' said his grandmother.

The postman came, and drank tea, sitting on a bench near the door.

'My grandson, from London,' she said.

'Never been there,' said the postman: 'never been out of Wales.'

His face, made by other generations, and by the land and the

86

mountains, was clear-skinned, like a child's.

She watched him go, and then said:

'Here's Colum coming.'

The boy was tall and dark, gipsy-looking, stringy, slightly apprehensive. He wore a blue polo-neck sweater, patched jeans, white socks and sneakers. He had to duck to come into the kitchen.

'A country of giants, that's what it'll be,' she said. 'This is Steven.'

They shook hands, clumsily.

'Tea?' she said.

'I wouldn't say no.'

'Where will you take him?' she said. 'Do you want to go out for the day, Steven?'

'We'll see how it goes.'

'You can come back for lunch here, if you like, Colum.'

'We'll see how it goes,' said Colum.

*

The gradient was punishing. Not wishing to show weakness, they battled on, swaying, gasping. To rest at a stone wall, mortared by moss. The only sound their breathing.

Colum swallowed, and pointed.

'Barn owl lives there,' he said. 'Want to go and see?'

'In a minute,' said Steven.

He turned and rested his back against the wall. It seemed to finger his spine. Hard, bony fingers. He pushed himself off. Down below, light glared off a lake. The cries of sheep came from afar, plaintive.

They left the bikes at the wall and crossed the rough field. The barn was old and no longer used: the same moss was winning. Inside, the high roof soared to shadowy rafters, a scatter of sun where slates had slipped.

'See it?' said Colum.

'No.'

'Up there. In the corner.'

It was a blue-whiteness, hooded, yet watching.

Steven reached to the floor and picked up a stone.

'What are you going to do?' said Colum.

87

'Shift it. See it fly.'

'I should leave it alone.'

'You're not me.'

'You might hit it.'

'So?'

But he dropped the stone. He looked around. Tramps had slept here, used the place. Old stained newspapers, threadbare sacks, seeds that had taken hold, thriving.

'Big deal,' he said. 'Come to Wales for the big deal.' He followed Colum out into the light. They sat against the wall of the barn. 'You always lived in the country?'

'No. I'm from Manchester.'

'Why here?'

'My father's idea. A new life, he says.'

'Ha. Bet you miss Manchester.'

'It was a dump,' said Colum. 'I wouldn't go back. You ever seen Moss Side?' He looked at Steven. 'Not going to work, is it?'

'What?'

'This. You don't want to go around with me, do you?'

'No.'

'I knew as soon as I saw you.'

'Nothing personal,' said Steven. 'Old ladies like to fix things. I won't be here a week. I'm bored out of my skull already. I'll think of something. Sorry.'

'Fair enough,' said Colum. 'I'll go, then. There's plenty I can do. Just came as a favour . . .'

'Right,' said Steven. 'See you.'

Colum got up and walked across the field to the stone wall. Steven watched him move smoothly down the hill, the bike seen for an instant when the wall crumbled and dropped, before it rose again.

Crows or rooks called from high trees, black among untidy nests. There were small bones among the grassblades.

Steven went back inside the barn. The owl was in the same place, at the end of the rafter. Steven picked up the stone.

'Come on, you old sod!' he shouted. 'Move!'

The throw, powered by frustration, was too accurate. The stone hit the owl in the face. The bird gave a cry, part whistle part squeak, and fell. Nearing the floor, it recovered, and veered towards Steven. He ducked, fear stopping his breath, and the wings beat inches from his head, and away. He ran to the door. The owl seemed to limp through the air, going low over the field. It clung to the top of the stone wall, rocked, spread its wings again, and flew towards the wood.

When Steven got to the wall, a spot of blood was drying into the topmost stone.

*

He stayed out all morning, riding the lanes, resting on walls and in fields. In a village shop he bought cigarettes and matches, and a bus-timetable. Hunger drew him back to the farm around one o'clock.

His parents were sitting outside the house, in deckchairs, on the small daisy-whitened lawn. A wind came down from the mountain, shook the thick yew tree, and moved on down the valley.

'You've caught the sun,' said his mother. 'Hasn't he, Joe?'

'Sweating like a pig,' said his father. 'Get some of that flab off.'

'How was the boy?' she said.

'Okay. Have you had lunch?'

'Yes. Yours is inside. A nice ham salad.'

He washed at the kitchen sink and used the striped towel.

'Get on all right with Colum?' said his grandmother, taking the cover off the salad.

'Yes thanks.'

His grandfather, feet up on a low stool, prepared for his customary nap.

'Take you up to see the sheep, after,' he said. 'If you like.'

'I'm seeing Colum again this afternoon, Pop,' he said.

'Any time, son,' said the old man. He turned off his hearing-aid and closed his eyes.

Steven ate the salad. And then the sherry-trifle. And then the cheese and biscuits.

'Nice to see an appetite,' said his grandmother. 'And you've caught the sun.'

*

That night, weary and aching from a day's unaccustomed cycling, the sun still a burning mask on his face, he lay in a cool bed,

89

planning his return to London. Halfway through a thought, he fell into sleep.

Dream, nightmare, reality – he found himself sitting up. Heart pounding, face rinsed with sweat, battling with his breath, his head swung towards the window.

The owl was hovering between the stars and the glass. Its wings beat back and forth, a slow-motion suspension of time. Its flat face gleamed with blood. It opened its claw-like ivory beak and cried. But there was no sound. It was now so close to the glass that blood smeared the pane. Its claws began to scrape: the sound was like faint screams.

Steven pulled the covers over his head. Down there, in that black warmth, he could smell his own fear.

When he looked again, the owl had gone. The stars shone clear and cold. He got out of bed, switched on the light, and went to the window. There were no marks on the glass. Beyond the window the farm buildings were safe and sound.

Nightmare.

*

He had thought to get his grandmother on his side. But she was off to Brecon after breakfast, with his mother and father; and he found himself riding the tractor with his grandfather, the dogs crammed between them. The track was tortuous, at all angles, and the tractor leapt and jolted, the dogs slipping, scrambling back. Finally, they gave up, and ran alongside, fur feathered by the wind.

Between the valley and the mountain the sheep were gathered. Lambs stumbled after their mothers, and the air was full of their cries.

The dogs were difficult to control. They danced and spun, eager for work. The old man's voice sharpened, called them to order. But not for long.

Up against a wall a lone ewe tried to shield something.

'Back, Emma, damn you!' said the old man. '*Back!*'

The lamb was a bundle of blood and sinew, its eyes already taken.

'Hawk or fox,' said the old man. He got a piece of sacking from the tractor, wrapped the lamb, and put it on the seat. The ewe moved around the huge earth-grooved wheels, lost.

'Smoke, Pop?' said Steven.

'Gave 'em up a long time ago,' said his grandfather. His face fitted the land, was part of it, as were the sheep, the dead lamb, the diving black birds. 'Your mother know?

'Guesses, I suppose.'

'Not a good habit,' said the old man. He sniffed the blue smoke, and the old pleasure came back, but was denied.

'What will you do with the lamb?' said Steven.

'Dump it away from the mother. Something will finish it off.'

Steven leaned against the wheel. The ewe wandered around, lifting her head, searching.

'Pop,' he said: 'I want to go back to London.'

The old man looked down the slope at his sheep.

'Do what you like, son,' he said. 'Your gran will be disappointed. She has a few things planned.'

'But there's nothing to *do*,' said Steven.

'You got on all right with Colum.'

'That was a lie.'

'Oh,' said his grandfather.

'We had nothing in common. They'll be in Brecon most of the day. Do you think I could go now? I could get the eleven-ten bus, and catch the coach in . . . '

'I don't think that's a good idea,' said the old man. 'Sneaking off. Tell them this evening. Go tomorrow.'

'But they'll . . . '

'You don't like facing them, right? Well, you'll have to, boy. Are we that bloody terrible?'

*

Going back, they neared the wall, the field.

'Drop me off here, Pop,' said Steven. 'Colum says there's an owl in that barn.'

'Don't say something's interested you,' said his grandfather. 'There's hope for you yet.' The engine idled as Steven got down. The old man took the lamb from the sacking. 'Dump it behind the wall.'

The lamb was like a stiff puppet, streaked.

'I'll walk back,' said Steven.

'Something and oven chips. Corned beef?'

'That'll be great.'

The tractor throbbed away, the dogs happy with more room.

Steven dropped the lamb in the long grass behind the wall, and wiped his hands on his jeans.

Approaching the barn, he paused. Something of the night's strangeness still clung to his brain. What if a bloodied face waited for him? He went in.

The rafter was empty. There were a few speckled feathers resting lightly on the dust. Where was it now? But what did it matter? A dead owl was the same as a dead lamb. *Something will finish it off.*

Returning, he saw a bird rise from the lamb and position itself further along the wall. A few paces down the hill, he looked back. The bird was gone.

*

Alone in the house, watching the TV, the camera tracking along the Thames, he heard the car in the courtyard.

They came in.

'Oh, for a cup of tea!' said his mother. 'Put the kettle on, Steven. How can you watch TV on such a lovely evening . . . '

He went into the kitchen and filled the kettle. He plugged it in and went back into the living-room. His grandfather was shucking off his boots at the open door. The dogs, splayed out on warm flagstones, watched him.

Steven's grandmother lifted a bag from among others, and opened it. She took out a sweater, shook it open, and held it in front of her.

'This is for you, Steven,' she said. 'Haven't bought you anything in years.'

The sweater was tropic-blue, and a stitched gull spread its wings across the chest.

He began to thank her, but his grandfather spoke first.

'He wants to go home,' he said.

It was unnecessarily cruel to say it now: now with the sweater held out, a gift. The old man's face was stern: an unexpected hurt had given voice.

His grandmother held the sweater against her: a flimsy shield.

'Home?' she said. 'Already?'

'Of course he doesn't,' said her daughter. 'He's only joking, Pop. Don't worry, Mum.'

'He'd have gone this morning if I'd have let him,' said the old man, slipping into his house shoes.

Steven's grandmother gave him the sweater.

'I'll go and make the tea,' she said.

Pop sat in his chair and watched the news.

'What's the matter with you, Steven?' said his father. 'Christ, can't you give anyone some of your time?'

'And Gran helping you with that boy . . . ' said his mother.

'He was a dumbo,' said Steven.

'They're all dumbos according to you. I don't want to play the heavy father . . . '

'About time you did, Joe,' she said.

' . . . and I don't often insist – but I do now. You're here until Saturday, so make the most of it.'

His grandmother brought in the tray.

'And we're going on a day-trip to Colwyn Bay on Thursday,' she said. 'It's all booked. You always liked it there, Steven.'

The carrot of a day at the coast, which heightened his childhood, made no impression now. The sea would limp in, hardly lifting the tangled weed in the rockpools; and the same man in the striped apron would be there, standing under the striped flapping awning, selling tea in thick white mugs, handing over cakes whose pink icing cracked under your teeth, and whose sickly taste you never forgot.

He would go tomorrow. He would find a way.

'Yes, Gran,' he said.

She smiled. She liked things plain and simple: like nature.

'Try it on, Steven,' she said.

He was covered in a smell of newness. His head emerged. She tugged the sweater into place.

'There,' she said. 'Just the right size. Look at yourself.'

He turned obediently to the large gold-framed mirror by the door. He *had* caught the sun: he looked like an advert for a ski-resort or a coast running with surf and topless girls.

'Say thank you to your Gran,' said his mother.

'Thanks very much, Gran,' he said.

'Now, we'll have no more talk about going home, will we?'
'No, Gran,' he said.

THREE

Night came, and again that terrible dream.

The owl was back, outside the window, flat white face bloodied, beak open in that soundless cry, wings slowly beating, yet a blur.

He stared at it. It seemed intent on breaking in. In the dream he got out of bed and ran to the window. Smears on the glass. He read hatred in eyes that held his own reflection. He wrenched the window open. It thudded to the top of the frame. Night air came in off the mountain, cool on his sweat. There was nothing there: just the still, watchful courtyard; the farm buildings complete with shadows; the mountain's shoulder against the stars. No fox yelped, no sheep bleated on the dark hill, all creation watched, or slept.

He stood there, breathing in the cool air. The panic in his heart subsided. He went back to bed.

*

He woke again, near dawn.

His feet were hurting: a kind of hot cramp. He put his hands down. The flesh burned. He reached out and felt for the bedside lamp. His toes were bunching. He threw back the covers.

The lamp's light was kind: a warm orange. He looked down. Between his toes a whiteish fluff was growing, like a special mould. He touched it. It was the most delicate thing in the world. His toes thinned and hardened. The talons came, newly-made, precise, as his own nails shrivelled. His ankles began to fuzz in quick layers of small feathers. He thudded his back into the pillow, his open mouth against that starched grandmother's smell, urging the dream to finish, to leave.

But it was no dream. Even as his face lifted for air, he felt his whole body begin to fold in on itself. Feathers rushed from his legs and began to pattern his stomach. His heart shrank to a bird's heart: a quick, rapid flutter. Everything was contracting. The

94

bold wings sheathed his infant arms. His face lost all humanity. The mouth pursed to a beak, hard as bone. The eyes widened. The ears faded under tufts. He gave one last human cry, which was never finished, or heard.

*

The bird moved in the bed, terrified of the folds that held it. It struggled free and roamed the room with the whisper of its wings. Every sense alive, it felt the pressure of air from the window. It found the space, and launched itself into the night.

It rested on a post near the chicken-run. The dogs heard the shuttle of wings, but did not stir. The bird groomed itself, there in the coming dawn. It lifted its head, hearing every sound. It gave a hungry cry, and lifted itself to the hill.

Flying over the barn, it caught the smell of death. Something was close to the wall. The owl sighed down and landed close to the dead lamb. It began to tear at what remained, feeding on dry sinew, the last meat.

*

Warm morning air filled the barn. The owl slept on the rafter: a white completeness spotted by sunlight. Its talons gripped, its wings folded, its speckled chest rose and fell. It breathed.

Something woke it, swiftly. It opened its eyes. Inched a little along the rafter. Looked down.

Its enemy had entered. The owl moved into the shadow, the angle of the roof. It gripped the flaking wood.

*

Then something came racing up towards it. It hit the bird full in the face. The owl fell back against the roof.

It cried, once.

Then tried for the mountain, the free air.

95

The White Horses Of The Sea

I was never the beer-swilling roustabout poet, the golden terror of the circuits, vomiting in a corridor before an evening's reading at some Middle-America campus, a new legend every five minutes, dying in a coma or diving from a bridge or choking on a peach-stone. I do not like the unbuttoned.

But I did have to sell my soul. About once a month, to keep a roof over my head, and that of she who worked part-time, increasingly dubious of long-promised reward: the TV profile, a Poetry Society Choice, the Nobel. We all dream, seeing lesser men than ourselves caught lucky. Adjudications mostly: the parcel of misshapen papers: atrocious typing, spidery handwriting, conventional themes and emotions, outpourings; never a new thought, a new eye. There was a time when I was interested, hoping to discover, nurture, a talent, a freshness. But then it became a burden, a bore. I winced at the postman's smile.

Poetry Weekends at a country house. A new one: Parton Hall, outside Guildford. A fee, travelling expenses, the customary room over tended gardens. Once I was flattered: no more.

Younger, I had hoped for a kindred soul: some beauty among the yews, stepping out, instantly recognisable. Never. Always the woollen brigade, the lonely elderly scribblers, or the over-earnest young believing all the legends, regarding one as the envied published, the name on the jacket, the face on the back flap: an old photograph, when *I* was earnest.

Introduced in the sunlit room, I smiled at the applause.

The faces were different, but were all aspects of the same person: the desperate Versifier. Desperate to be read, applauded, consoled, led, patted, advised, printed. In each large handbag or briefcase a file held their life's-blood, eager to be spilled.

Nothing was new: I had been here a hundred times, even in another life – it felt that long.

There was one remotely possible. In her thirties. I liked the freedom of her bare arms. Drinking instant coffee, we listened to our words whilst invisible hands moved. Mrs Scott-Forbes. A poet.

'Is your wife here?' she said.

'No – she's heard it all before.'

'Ah.'

The leader of the weekend, a Georgian poet grown old, gave me my burden.

It was housed in a thick blue folder. Sitting on my bed in the clean room, I took out the pages. The first, on yellow paper, was "The New Crucifixion". Modern man pinned by electronics. I moved to the next. "After The Bomb". The scarred cities, the cry of a single survivor. Man endures . . .

I lay back on the bed. Leaf-shadows moved on the ceiling, and outside on the lawn a woman laughed.

I fell asleep; but, waking, turned to my duty.

*

It was then I knew that this must be my last. The fee, the faint ego-trip, this room, that garden: nothing was worth these . . . insults. We would endure without the folded cheque.

Cats, birds, seasons, love, pain, death, ecstasy, roses, wilderness, Christ, Edens, ice, heat, forests, the wonder of birth: these were last year's efforts and the year before. The same cries and shouts, a continuous echo. I battled on, making notes thick with exclamations. Had no one ever skinned their eyes? Messages from the grave. I thought fire a beautiful cleanser, the purity of ashes.

> The White Horses Of The Sea
> Jesus!
> *How they roar in, the white horses of the sea!*
> *Manes of water, hoofs of weed.*
> *Pawing the sand, retreating, leaving shells*
> *As gifts!*
> *Stallions, mares of green, foals following*
> *In the surf.*
> *Here they come again, endless herds.*

Such were the horses of my childhood:
Endlessly coming.
A promise.
They never leave me —
My green children.

None of the poems were signed. Anonymous, their creators awaited my thoughts, opinions, decision: there were two prizes.

I hoped Mrs Scott-Forbes was innocent of "The White Horses Of The Sea". I looked at the next. "My Grandfather". The open mouth, the spittle, came on the third line.

*

The Georgian Poet came in. He carried a bottle of whisky and two glasses.

'Thought we might mellow before supper.'

'Fine.'

Evening had darkened the room, and I switched on a second light. He poured the drinks, and I watered mine from the basin in the corner.

'Cheers,' he said. 'Good hunting.'

I saluted his white head, and moved to the armchair. He nodded at the pages on the bed.

'Found any nuggets?'

'No,' I said, and heard the despair in my voice. 'Have you?'

'No,' he said. 'You sound . . . aggressive.'

'A natural reaction.'

He sipped at his whisky.

'Done many of these weekends, have you?' he said.

'Too many.'

'Your standards are high.'

'I like to think so.'

'Are you bringing out a new collection?'

'No plans for one. You?'

He waved a freckled hand.

'Who wants the fag-end of an old man's life?'

'You see yourself as a teacher, then? Adviser?'

Wounded, he drank some more.

'Don't let that aggression spill over. Don't be too hard on them.

Remember your own first efforts. All people need is encouragement. And they pay your fee.'

'This will be my last,' I said. 'It scares me: the thousands beavering away . . . To what end?'

'To provide you – and me – with employment. So the *real* work can get written.

'I suppose I deserve that.'

'We have to make a crust somehow,' he said. 'The fact that they can take their eyes off TV is ground enough for hope. Send them away happy, that's all they ask.' He lifted the bottle. 'Another?'

'No thanks.'

*

All their eyes at supper. Their bright moist interest. *Have you had a chance to read our work, Mr Gaines?*

All will be revealed tomorrow.

I was the possessor of a great secret: if listened to intently enough its tail-end might be caught, pulled by a comet into stardom.

I had to give my group an assignment: to be completed the following afternoon. They waited expectantly, pens at the ready.

' "Spectacles",' I said.

Dismayed, the light went from their faces.

'What sort of spectacles?' said the bearded one.

'I say no more,' I said, and stood from the round table, the litter of glasses and ashtrays.

'About how long?' said another.

'"Spectacles",' said Mrs Scott-Forbes. 'It has potential. Yes.'

'As long or as short as you like,' I said. 'If you'll excuse me . . . '

'We thought of going down to the pub . . . ' said the beard.

'No thank you,' I said.

'I thought you might stay and talk to us,' said a small, tidy grey-haired woman. 'We all need so much help. I know I do . . . Where to send our work . . . '

'Workshop's tomorrow afternoon,' I said. I looked at Mrs Scott-Forbes, and moved away. 'Goodnight.'

She followed me into the hall and made for the stairs.

'I thought a stroll before bed . . . ' I said.

'I'll get my coat.'

'It's a warm night.'

'But deceptive,' she said.

She left the coat unbuttoned. It swayed around her like a cloak. We climbed the hill in silence and rested on a farm-gate. There was a glow in the sky that was Guildford. A warm yeasty smell came off the field. The shape of her head was black against the stars.

'I found a copy of your first book the other day,' she said, speaking to the black field. '*Ghostship.* I brought it along for you to sign.'

'Where on earth did you find that?'

'In Charing Cross road. It was remaindered.'

'Thank you.'

'But so was Eliot and Berryman. You were in good company. You were very young, then.'

'It showed.'

'I liked "The Desert Blooms The Cactus" best of all. There was joy there.'

'Have you submitted a poem called "The White Horses Of The Sea"?'

She turned to face me. But her face was unrecognisable in the dark.

'Aren't we to remain anonymous?'

'*Have* you?'

'I'm not telling you. Has it won?.'

'You won't tell me?'

'Why should I be so favoured? Let it be a surprise.'

'Are you happily married?'

'I can't have children.'

'Is that an answer?'

'Part of one. Have *you* children?'

'One son. At East Anglia. What does your husband do?'

'Redundant executive. Has a passion for folk-dancing. He's on a course this weekend. We compare notes.'

'I like your arms.'

She drew the coat around her and buttoned it.

'Shall we go back?' she said. 'And you're being young again.'

*

After breakfast everyone gathered in the Blue Room. All were rested and showered and fed, and dressed in bright casuals. I had made one concession: no jacket, but still kept the tie. The Georgian Poet and myself were to read the poems in turn, and comment. The prizes to be awarded at the end. We sat behind a table on a raised platform. The carafe of water caught the light, sent rainbow lances across my folder. Ahead of us, behind the poets, the garden was clear and sharp in the sun.

'Shall I begin?' he said.

I nodded, not caring. My prize-winners were tosses of a coin.

He stood up.

'Are we ready then?'

The talk died and the expectant faces lifted. The need to be noticed. To be seen apart from the crowd. The creators.

'I shall start with "Florentine Holiday",' he said. 'A poem of four stanzas. The rhyme-scheme is ambitious, to say the least. But what would life be without a challenge?'

He cleared his throat. His legs bumped the table, and the lances shifted.

> *St. Francis is here in every face,*
> *Heritage of love the poor devour . . .*

And then he said:

'Mr Gaines . . . ? Would you care to comment?'

He had read the poem and given his opinion: I had heard only the garden, the monotonous, repeated calling of an unknown bird.

'No, I think you covered it very well.'

'Will you continue then, please?'

I stood up and took out "The New Crucifixion".

> *These are not nails that hold you now, modern Jesus;*
> *Your crown no longer thorns . . .*

*

I had taken his advice and been kind. But my kindness was as nothing to his bland reassurance, his laying on of hands. He found something to praise in every bone-aching poem, every conventional response. *Nice touch there: the sundial's shadow*

*evoking death. The slight fuzz of hair on the child's face –
peachlike – good. A map of wrinkles – yes.*

And my next was "The White Horses Of The Sea".

Standing, I held it in my hands. Over their heads the bird still
called. For what reason – that unvarying cry?

I looked at them, human like yourself. One of them had
perpetrated "The White Horses". Who . . . ? It did not matter.
Away with kindness: let's be honest.

The White Horses Of The Sea I said. And read it, slowly.

'I'll read it once again.' And did so.

I lifted my head and looked at their faces. Three were smiling;
all were intent. The bird sang on.

'That is a terrible poem,' I said.

There was a gasp of concern.

'It is possibly the worst poem we shall hear this weekend. It is
unfelt, uninspired, shallow, a repeating of a cliché. How many of
you have seen waves as white horses?'

Every hand went up.

'What is poetry?' I said. I thought of all I had tried to do,
remaindered. 'It's a skinning of the eyes. It's a door opening
where you thought there was no door. It's a revelation, an insight.
What revelation is here? What insight? The door has opened, but
what's behind it? A common thought, no more.'

'But waves coming in *do* look like horses,' said the bearded
one. 'What was it?: *mares of green, endless herds?* Nothing
wrong with that.'

There was a murmur of agreement.

'Nothing wrong with it . . . ?'

The Georgian Poet touched my sleeve.

'I feel sure Mr Gaines doesn't want to get involved in a class
discussion now. We simply haven't the time.'

'We have the time,' I said. 'I won't be long. This poem is bad
because nothing leaps out and grabs you. Shakes you alive. It is
boring because it goes no deeper than a stock response. Of course
waves give the impression of flowing manes. But it's a tired, dead
image. Like faces in clouds: we all see them, nothing exceptional.
I want something to enrich my life, a *newness*. Here we only nod
agreement – say yes, that's how we saw it once, twice, ad infini-
tum. . . forever. The person who wrote this is lazy, complacent. . .'

The small, tidy, grey-haired woman in the second row was tugging at her handkerchief, her eyes blurred with tears. She stood up.

'Excuse me,' she said in a choked voice, and pushed her way to the end of the row, and hurried out of the room. The door closed.

There was a silence. All eyes were on my face.

'Now you know who wrote it,' said Mrs Scott-Forbes. 'Satisfied?'

'Going a bit strong, weren't you?' said the bearded one. 'We aren't all geniuses like you, you know.'

'Mr Gaines was right,' said a woman: 'it was a pretty awful poem. She . . . '

'He could have let her down easier,' said a man who had a red face and a paunch. He shifted on his chair. 'We come here to be helped, not railroaded.'

'I didn't know she had written it,' I said.

'Does that matter?' said the Georgian Poet. 'I'm sure Mr Gaines will make amends: be more *constructive*. Shall we continue? We're nearing break-time . . . My next is "High Sierra" . . . '

I sat down.

*

She did not appear for coffee. The poets were free to work on their assignments, until lunch. Workshops would begin at 2:30.

'What number is her room?' I asked Mrs Scott-Forbes. 'I'll take her some coffee.'

'That's the least you can do, you butcher,' she said. 'Twelve, second floor.'

I knocked and waited. The coffee steamed. One of the biscuits was crumbling.

No answer. I opened the door. The untidy room was empty. A faint smell of perfume.

'Mrs Mason?' I said. The words hung in the air.

I went downstairs again and gave the coffee and the biscuits to one of the kitchen staff.

'Nothing wrong with it, is there?' she said.

'No,' I said: 'someone decided against a second cup.'

I went out of the house. The sun was strong for October: all smells baked dry. The poets were stretched out on the lawns. Most were asleep, or thinking. Those with open eyes ignored me. I saw my own cruelty, and winced.

A small whitestone bridge, more decorative than functional, crossed a mossy stream. Flies sang, fed on my sweat. She was sitting on the far bank, resting against a tree, eyes closed.

I came up, quietly.

'Mrs Mason?'

Startled, she jerked her head. Her face had a raw, washed quality.

'Go away please,' she said.

I sat beside her. Together we looked at the stream, the haze of insects.

'I'm sorry,' I said.

'It's too late now.'

'I'm sorry to have upset you.'

'You did more than that.'

I was silent. I put my hands either side of me. One brushed young thistles, and the barbs stung.

'You *know* what you did?' she said.

Her stare was fierce, unforgiving.

'You killed that poem,' she said. 'You took it and tore it to pieces. You killed the memory of that day. When I had that . . . *stock response*. I don't want to be in your group. I'll transfer to Mr Lovell's.'

'You won't,' I said. 'Mrs Mason – it's a bad poem. We've all written them. There's no disgrace. We learn . . . '

'It was published in our local paper,' she said. 'I had some letters . . . '

'Mrs Mason, what do you see? Here. Over there. Describe what you see.'

'I don't want to.'

'Do you see trees in russet dresses? Leaves the colour of old coins? A silver-bubbled stream? You see what I'm getting at?'

'I *will* transfer,' she said. She got up and brushed her skirt. 'You want the world according to *you*, Mr Gaines. I've read some of your poems. Mrs Scott-Forbes has one of your books. I didn't recognise anything. I wasn't moved a bit.'

'Not even to anger?' I said.

'I wouldn't be that inconsiderate,' she said. 'Some of us have standards. We know how to behave.'

She picked the last leaf off the cloth and walked to the bridge.

I lay on my back and put my hands under my head. The clouds were high and wispy. That one looked like Merlin, the beard.

*

Someone sat beside me. It was Mrs Scott-Forbes. She was cool and fresh, bare-armed. Shadows moved over her.

'She's transferring to Lovell,' I said.

'Some of the others aren't too sure, either.'

'And you?'

'I won the prize. I couldn't be that disloyal.'

I turned my body and looked at the fuzz of her arms.

'Aren't you into folk-dancing?'

'No. I want some help with "Spectacles" . . . '

She turned the pages of her pad.

I ran my finger down her arm.

'How far have you got?'

'It's very rough . . . '

'Go on.'

> *In every size they come: our windows on the world.*
> *Prescribed, or bought on market stalls*
> *They bring the ordinary closer, no longer*
> *Ordinary . . .*

She paused.

'All right, so far?'

I lay on my back, took her left hand and squeezed her fingers.

'Great,' I said. 'Go on.'

> *Here is an old man, eyes dimmed with age . . .*

*

That one looked like a castle, before it changed. And that, a white horse, mane flying.

THE HOCKEY-PLAYER

ONE

Warm in the car, heading home, listening to an Elgar tape, he heard a death-rattle from the engine. The momentum took him out of the fast lane and on to the hard shoulder. And there it died.

The cello played on in the silence. He switched it off. He knew little about the interior of cars. The lines mattered, the latest model; and there were always other men who knew. He pressed the button to release the bonnet, and got out.

Cold came off night-filled farmland and pounced. The last days of October; winter coming. Other more efficient cars swept by. He shivered. He lifted the bonnet and the light came on. There was a strong smell of petrol and hot oil. Everything looked normal. He poked a few wires.

He got back into the car and tried to start the engine. Nothing.

Other men had told him you never break down near a motorway-phone, but he was lucky: he found one within a hundred yards, its black hood glistening with moisture. The cold, inhuman touch on his ear.

The voice was hardly warmer, as if he had interrupted something.

He explained what had happened.

' . . . on the M6, south of Stafford . . . '

'We know your position,' said the voice. 'Are you north or south of the phone?'

'South.'

'They'll be there in fifteen minutes.'

'Thank you.'

Elgar no longer fitted the occasion. It seemed frivolous, a candied border to life. Silence was better, watching headlamps and tail-lights coming and going. The car grew colder.

The yellow truck drew alongside, bright warning lamps spinning. The two mechanics joined him at the open bonnet. A powerful smell of cigarettes clung to their overalls.

'Don't stand around in the cold, sir,' said the older man. 'Be with you in a minute.'

Edwardes went back. Shivering, he held on to the wheel.

The older man slipped beside him.

'Fuel-pump's gone sir. Have to tow you to the garage. Where you making for?'

The cigarette-smell was like another physical presence.

'Holmes Chapel,' said Edwardes.

'Can't do anything for you tonight. It'll be ready tomorrow afternoon. You could get a train from Stafford to Crewe. There's one just before midnight.'

'That seems the best solution.'

'Right, sir. Sit tight.'

Edwardes winced as the tow-bar was fitted: the clanging, the bruising.

The mechanic waved in the headlamps, spot-lit, like an actor.

The car jolted forward, disgraced.

*

The garage was bleak under powerful arc-lamps.

'Take your particulars, can I, sir?' said the older man, shortened in this light to a creature of oil and grey hair. He held the clip-board ready.

'Here's my card,' said Edwardes. 'You can reach me at my office tomorrow. May I use your phone?'

'Help yourself, sir.'

He stood among files, road-maps and girlie calendars, and imagined her waking in the dark bedroom . . .

'Yes?' she said, and her voice was made of sleep.

'It's Frank, Hilda.'

'Frank? Where are you?'

'I've broken down on the motorway . . . '

'But the car's brand-new.'

'I know. Broken fuel-pump. I'll have to come back by train to Crewe, and get a taxi from there.'

'Oh, what a bind,' she said. 'Are you all right?'

'Yes. Go back to sleep.'

'I've left a snack under cover in the kitchen.'

'Kids okay?'

'I've kept James home another day. It's still on his chest, and the coughing . . . '

'Right. It'll be one-ish, about.'

'All right, Frank. Take care.'

He held the coin out to the mechanic.

'That's all right, sir. All part of the service.'

'No, I'd rather pay. How do I get to Stafford Station?'

'Pete'll run you there. Pete, run this gentleman to the station. And no calling in at the chippy.'

*

As the station sign and the arrow came out of the night, Edwardes said, in the fog:

'How many do you smoke a day?'

'Forty, fifty.' The cigarette bobbed. 'Depends.'

'Don't you think of your health?'

'When you go, you go. Stressful job, right? If you'd seen some of the sights I've seen . . . You ever smoked?'

'Never,' said Edwardes. 'I've more respect for my lungs.'

'You pull a burned body out of a wreck, you'd smoke,' said the young mechanic. The ash fell on his stained trousers. 'That'll be a fiver. Cost you more in a taxi.'

Edwardes paid, standing in cold, smoke-free air. And watched the car leave the forecourt, his throat burning.

TWO

He had not used a train in years. Or a bus or the Tube. Cocooned in cars and taxis and executive-class planes, he now felt lost and strangely vulnerable in acres of night-shadowed concrete. The lights were those of a prison or a concentration-camp, his own shadow enormous.

'Twenty minutes,' said the man in the ticket-office.

Edwardes went through to the platform. Near midnight, every-thing was closed, unlit. A wind pushed through the station, and

109

the lit lamps swayed, sending ovals of light scurrying. Spaced out on the platform, their positions measured, were two men. One was a blind man, his guide-dog a brown-black shape at his feet. The other, nearer to Edwardes, was a young man carrying a plastic carrier-bag and a hockey-stick. The blind man's head was lifted slightly, as though he tasted the silence. The other glanced at Edwardes, and away.

A distinct unease grew in Edwardes. He could not say why, but he became fearful. A station at night, silence, swaying lamps, a blind man and a resting dog, a youngster with a hockey-stick. He shook himself. Crazy bastard. He smiled in his cold face. But it did not help.

The young man with the hockey-stick moved. He walked towards Edwardes, and passed him, looking straight ahead. Returning, he glanced at Edwardes and away.

Nothing was said, and again he took up his measured position.

The signal light changed to green. Far down the track the train appeared, a single white eye.

Edwardes walked to the blind man. The dog stirred and the white frame shifted.

'What is it, Peg?' said the blind man. 'Is it coming?'

'It's coming,' said Edwardes. 'Do you want some help?'

Under a thatch of coarse hair the blind man's eyes were moist and empty of life. Light swayed over his face.

'Kind of you,' he said. 'Just see us to a second-class.'

A porter appeared, rubbing his hands.

'You're out late,' said Edwardes to the blind man.

'Why should that surprise you?' said the blind man.

'I just thought . . .'

'Are we incapable?'

'No, I'm sorry.'

'Thinks we're incapable, Peg.'

The train came smoothly in. Most of its passengers were asleep. One person got off. Edwardes helped the blind man to a second-class seat. The dog settled itself under the table, sighed, and closed its eyes.

'Where are you going?' said Edwardes.

'Manchester,' said the blind man. 'You've got a voice that says first-class. Thank you.'

As Edwardes walked to the first-class section, the train moved. The lights of the station were replaced by the lights of houses and stores. Then the black of the land.

He passed empty compartment after empty compartment. Only one was occupied: a fat man slept among scattered papers.

Almost at the rear of the train, he pulled open a door and closed it behind him. He put his briefcase in the rack, took off his overcoat, folded it, and put it next to the briefcase. He pulled down the sleeves of his jacket, and sat at the window-seat. The black countryside streamed by.

It was very warm in the train. A travelling hot-house. He turned the heating to *Off*, loosened his tie, and undid the top button of his shirt. He thought of home, of bed, of putting his arm around his wife . . .

The young man with the hockey-stick passed the door.

Edwardes no longer felt tired. All senses alert, he sat up. The unease returned. He looked at the door's reflection in the window.

The young man came back, and the door was opened. Edwardes still watched the reflection, threaded by the lights of cars. He saw the man sit down. The noise of the train, that steady pulsing, was another kind of silence.

Edwardes' neck, held in the same rigid position, began to ache. The young man moved and sat opposite him. Edwardes turned his head and looked at him.

Short, cropped black hair on a white bony face. Small ears, large hollowed eyes, large mouth that held a tentative smile. Thin body in a blue, white-striped windcheater over a black, button-down shirt. Thick belt with a snake-clasp on pale-blue flared trousers. White socks, blue sneakers. The plastic bag said *Shop at Murry's: The Scene Store*. Resting on it at an angle was the hockey-stick: old, with many indentations.

'Good evening,' said the young man.

The voice was quiet, and yet provocative. Provoking . . . what?

'Good evening,' said Edwardes. He wished now he had taken the seat by the door.

'Going far?'

111

'Crewe.'

'Me, too.'

'Excuse me,' said Edwardes, and stood.

'Oh, don't do that . . .'

'Do what?'

'You were going to get something from the rack. Are you embarrassed?'

'About what?'

'Talking to me.'

'No.'

'Well, don't get anything down. We can talk till Crewe, can't we? It's not far.'

Edwardes sat down again.

'Thank you. What's your name?'

'Does it matter?'

'Mine's Raymond. Raymond Rowe. Come on, now.' He began to sing. '*We may never ever meet again on the rocky road to love . . .*'

'I don't think it's necessary,' said Edwards.

'You won't tell me?'

'No.'

'Well, then, I shall have to give you one.' Raymond considered him, leaning forward. 'You look like a . . . Patrick. Or a Richard. Getting warmer, am I?'

'No.'

'I shall have to call you Patrick.' Raymond held out a thin white hand. 'Pleased to meet you, Patrick.'

Edwardes looked above the hand to Raymond's face: that watchful friendliness. The train was going very fast. Crewe would soon race out of the dark. And then home . . .

He took the hand. It was smooth and warm.

'It's Frank,' he said.

A slight pressure.

'Hallo, Frank. You don't look a Frank. Do I look a Raymond?'

'I wouldn't know.'

Raymond sat back.

'Had a good day, Frank?'

'Not bad.'

'What do you do?' said Raymond, settling himself into the

corner. 'No, let me guess. I like guessing.'

'You were wrong with Patrick.'

'Bank manager. Solicitor? Accountant?'

'No.'

'Surprise me. Firewalker?'

Edwardes smiled, became a little less tense.

'I work for a chemical company.'

'Scientist?'

'Administrative.'

'Why so late?

'I've been attending a conference. What do you do?'

'I hated Science at school,' said Raymond. 'The smells. The dissecting. Poor bloody frogs, rabbits. Art was my best subject. Could have got an A Level at that, if I'd stayed.'

A high, travelling whistle sounded, and a train passed in the opposite direction. It too looked empty.

'And now?' said Edwardes.

'Your turn to guess,' said Raymond, and took up a pose.

Edwardes studied the tilted head, the stance.

'Drama school?' he said.

'No.'

'I'm no good at this sort of thing.'

'One more.'

'. . . hockey pro.'

Raymond laughed.

'No.'

'But you have been playing?'

'No. I'm not the sporty type.'

'Then why . . .?'

Raymond leaned over the carrier-bag and picked up the stick.

'It's a weapon,' he said.

*

He turned the stick in his hands.

'Don't get worried,' he said.

Edwardes began to feel cold. He switched on the heating and warm air began to beat at his ankles.

'A weapon?' he said.

'I'm a baker, see?' said Raymond. 'Unsocial hours, shift work.

Never know what crazy bastards you might meet. Can't carry a knife. No one minds a hockey-stick. Until it hits them.'

'I see it's been used.'

Raymond picked at the splintered end.

'This? No, it's secondhand. Never used it yet. Always ready, though.' He kissed the rough wood. 'Old faithful Horace. I call it Horace. Get it? Horace Hockey-stick.' He put it down. 'You got the time, Frank?'

Edwardes pushed back his sleeve.

'Ten past twelve.'

Raymond leaned forward.

'Looks a nice watch,' he said. 'Gold?'

'Yes.'

'Can I see it?'

Edwardes held out his wrist.

'No, I mean, can you take if off? Don't you trust me?'

'On one condition,' said Edwardes: 'I hold Horace.'

Raymond picked up the stick.

'Here.'

The stick across his thighs, Edwardes took off the watch. Raymond took it, and turned towards the light.

'Beautiful,' he said. 'Cost you a packet, this.'

'My wife bought it for me.'

Raymond sat back, holding the watch in two hands.

'Oh, you're married?'

'Yes.'

'Any kids?'

'Two boys. Ten and eight.'

'Happily? I mean, happily married?'

'Yes.'

'I'll put it on for you,' said Raymond. With a swift movement he took the stick and put it on top of the carrier-bag, and as swiftly sat next to Edwardes. 'What's the matter? I got the plague, or something?'

Edwardes had moved instantly, pressing himself against the window.

'You . . . startled me.'

'Never used Horace in my life,' said Raymond. 'Hold out your hand.'

He came closer and began to fix the watch. A sweet, familiar smell came from his breath. Parma violets.

'There.'

'Thank you.'

Raymond fingered Edwardes' sleeve.

'Nice material.' Close to, his skin was without blemish. He rubbed his finger on the flesh of Edwardes' wrist. 'I'm gay. Did you guess that?'

*

Edwardes moved and sat in Raymond's place. Fear had narrowed his throat, and he coughed.

'Never entered my mind,' he said.

'Don't lie, Frank.'

'No, honestly . . .'

The fat man passed on his way to the toilet. His very normalcy made this confrontation more disturbing. Edwardes felt an inner self cry out. Raymond came forward.

'Have you ever been gay, Frank?'

'No, never. I told you: I'm happily married.'

'With two kids – I know. Makes no difference. It takes one to know one, Frank.'

'What does that mean?'

'People like us, Frank . . .'

'What do you mean: *people like us*?'

Raymond was very patient.

'People like us know the signs, Frank. I knew as soon as you came on the platform. You can't hide it. It's there.' He tapped Edwardes' knee with one finger. 'And you knew it, too – when you saw me, right?'

A crackle of static sounded above their heads.

'This is the guard, ladies and gentlemen. We are now approaching Crewe. Next stop, Crewe. Thank you.'

'May I have my seat back?' said Edwardes. 'I want to get my things.'

Raymond unzipped one of the windcheater pockets, took out a small notebook, and then a pencil. He wrote something, tore out the page, and held it forward.

'That's my address and phone number, Frank.'

Edwardes picked up the hockey-stick, stood, and held it above Raymond's head.

'Will you get out of my seat!'

The fat man returned. Glancing in, he was rooted.

'*Help!*' cried Raymond; and laughed. He stood up, pushed the torn page into Edwardes's top pocket, and opened the door.

'Rehearsing,' he said. 'Actors.'

The fat man breathed relief.

'Scared me there for a second,' he said. The long shunting yards of Crewe appeared behind him: red and green lights, long lines of empty silent trucks. 'Crewe,' said the fat man.

'Yes,' said Raymond.

Edwardes was already into his overcoat, buttoning it.

'You're not offended,' said Raymond.

'Just . . . get out of my way.' He took down his briefcase. 'Excuse me.'

Raymond did not move. There was a certainty about him: a knowledge of his place in the world.

'If you can't get me at home, try the bakery. Winslade's of Crewe. In the book.' He smiled. 'Or call in: the market-place. I make a good apple-turnover.' He laughed. 'Oh, come on, Frank: don't look so bloody serious.'

'I don't want to touch you,' said Edwardes. 'Will you please move?'

Raymond stood aside.

'My pleasure. See you again, Frank.'

Crewe was as deserted as Stafford: sane men in their beds.

Edwardes dropped into the back of the taxi. The driver closed his paperback and put it into the glove-compartment.

'Where to, sir?'

'Holmes Chapel.'

'That's made my evening, that,' said the driver. 'Been dead as a doornail.'

The car was warm and comfortable. As it swung into the road, Edwardes saw Raymond standing outside the station: the white shine of the carrier-bag, the uplifted hockey-stick.

The driver settled into the best fare of the evening. This, and then home.

'Had a good day, sir?' he said.

'Look,' said Edwardes: 'I'd rather not talk.'

'Okay, sir. You take it easy. Mind a bit of music?'

Edwards closed his eyes.

'No,' he said.

THREE

'The one with the white iron fence,' he said.

'I see it, sir.'

'There's a driveway, and then the courtyard to your left.'

The driver nodded.

The house was in darkness, save for the coachlight at the door. The engine ticked over as Edwardes opened his wallet.

'Make it the round ten,' he said.

'That's very nice of you, sir. Thank you. Good night.'

Edwardes stayed in the courtyard until the car had gone. Until the last sound. Total silence now. Only then did his shoulders drop. He breathed in the night air. It was good to be home.

The house was warm. The fire in the living-room still glowed. The cat stretched itself on the carpet and went to sleep again.

He went into the kitchen. The fluorescent-tubes steadied. Under a plate were cold cuts of beef, crisp celery and tomatoes. He took off his overcoat and jacket, and sat down at the table. He ate everything, finishing with a glass of milk.

Then he went upstairs, leaving darkness behind him. He looked in on his sons. They slept deeply, never stirring. He went to the bathroom, used the toilet, and then washed: towelling his face until it glowed.

Wearing fresh pyjamas, he got into bed. She moved.

'Everything all right?' she said, her voice husky with sleep.

He put his arm around her and moved into that warm, familiar position: his body against her back, his legs shaped by hers.

'Yes,' he said. 'Fine.'

*

He was in a London Underground train. He was reading a

newspaper. *When he rose to get off the train at St. James', he found he was naked. He held the newspaper around him, and ran. In the park, lovers were in the long grass. One was kissing the breasts of a blissful girl.*

He was clothed again: dark suit, briefcase. Sweating, thankful, he took the stairs to his Manchester office.

It was a changing-room, littered with discarded tracksuits, shorts and vests. Talk came from another room.

He opened the door.

In a great bath, set into the floor, naked men soaked. Most had erections.

Naked again, he was called forward . . .

In the living-room, a nude Raymond was playing with the cat. He . . .

*

He always woke at the same time. It was a matter of pride with him: six-thirty. He looked at the clock on the bedside-table: six-thirty. All was well.

He sat up and looked at familiar things in the bedroom: things he and she had accumulated over the years. The weight of the years – gladly borne. He moved past her dark hair to the curve of her face, and kissed her.

'I love you,' he said.

She turned her sleep-blurred face to him and smiled.

'That's nice to know,' she said.

At breakfast, the noise of the children above them, he said:

'You'll run me to the station, yes?'

'Why don't you walk?'

'*Walk?*'

'It's a nice morning. You need the exercise.'

'It's almost two miles.'

'Not if you use the footpath.'

'No thanks. I'll let you run me there.'

The boys burst into the kitchen, and he saw them as if for the first time: individuals he had created, future men. The rest was the usual happy confusion, a disciplining ending in laughter.

After breakfast, the boys ran to get their coats.

He put on his jacket.

'I'll have to go to Stafford this afternoon to collect the car,' he said. 'If it's not ready, I may be late back. I'll give you a ring. I'll leave the office as early as I can.'

The boys came back, chasing.

'In the car,' she said. 'Go!'

James, the younger, made himself cough.

'Do I *have* to go?' he said.

'You do,' she said. 'Move.'

Edwardes got into his overcoat.

The last of the yellow roses stood in a blue vase on the window-ledge. Beyond them, in pale sunlight, the boys were running to the garage. Using the kitchen scissors, she cut a single half-open bud, opened his overcoat, and threaded the stem through the lapel of his jacket.

She rested her hands on his chest, and looked up.

'There,' she said.

'Hilda,' he said.

'Yes.'

'Thanks for everything.'

'Telling me you love me, and now this. What's brought all this on?'

'Last night,' he said. 'Being away.'

She patted his chest. The paper rustled in his top pocket, and its edge appeared.

'What's this?' she said, and took it out.

'It's nothing,' he said. 'Throw it away.'

She opened it.

'An address in Stafford?' she said. 'And a phone number.'

He buttoned his overcoat.

'It's nothing.'

She put the paper to her nose and sniffed. Her smile was a straight line.

'Parma violets?' she said.

Last Instruction

As the instruction progressed, her kissing became more ardent.
Her tongue now sought mine, as, in the beginning, mine had so
avidly sought hers; and her face had begun to grow that drowsy,
sensual mask I had seen so often in other women. Yet she always
had enough control to pull away. As now.

'I think you should go now,' she said. 'You'll be late.'

'I don't think I can stand much more of this,' I said.

I covered the nipple-print of her blouse with my lips. She
moved away and swung her legs off the other side of the divan.
She looked in the tall mirror and straightened her skirt.

'It's as hard for me as for you,' she said. 'After tonight, I'll feel
different: more at ease. Won't you?'

'Yes.'

'Good,' she said, in her precise way that was part of her appeal:
my own life lacking all precision. 'We'll have some wine with the
casserole.'

'I'll bring some in.'

'I already have,' she said. 'To celebrate.' She turned around.
'You'll wash before you go, will you?'

'Don't I always?'

Mary, the Mother of God, in a plaster plaque above the
bathroom mirror, smiled. Maternally.

'Wish me luck,' I said.

Her smile did not change.

April was standing in the hall, my coat in one hand, her college
scarf in the other. Coat on, she looped the scarf around my neck.

'I don't approve of college scarves,' I said. 'All girls together;
reunions.'

'But it's warm,' she said. 'That's the point.'

She opened the front door. Standing on tiptoe, she kissed me,
lightly.

'The last time,' she said.

'Praise the Lord,' I said, and stepped out into the night.

*

There was a roaring wind. I was a Pied Piper, leading scores of running, whispering autumn leaves up the hill. Gaunt black trees were printed on the sky. When I was closer, they creaked. In the narrow path between the church and the house, the leaves attacked me: whirling about my head, falling back as I reached the porch.

I pulled the more determined from my hair, and rang the bell. I was putting the comb away when the housekeeper opened the door. A tall thin nun in rimless spectacles, collar and cuffs startlingly white against the black.

'Good evening, Sister,' I said.

'Good evening, Mr Bennett.'

She stood aside. How old? Late forties, early fifties? And never been kissed. (Or *had* she, in the warm grass, before God called?) Christ her only lover. Her white unused body. And what if there were no Christ, no glorious reunion?

Leaves scampered into the hall. She closed the door.

'You're wearing her scarf,' she said, as though it were a sin.

'Greater love hath no woman,' I said, and hung coat and scarf alongside several blacknesses.

I turned to the study.

'No, Mr Bennett,' she said: 'Father would like to see you in the living-room tonight. Second door on your left.'

I left her picking up the leaves, one by one, her robe a moving black circle.

Always that smell I would never forget: polish and a spicy undertow. Incense? Certainly a religious air, found nowhere else.

I knocked on the shiny brown panel.

'Come in,' he said.

He was alone. Or rather, he had no *human* company. The white cat, Caesar, lay like shaped snow in the valley of his lap. The room was panelled and well-lit. A good fire. Light winking on glass and porcelain. Christ above the fire: the Dali, the foreshortened cross. That surprised me: the modernity. A tall Mary in an alcove. A warm room, comfortable, secure.

Father Louis moved and the cat jumped down. It stretched, testing every sinew.

'A windy night, Joseph,' said the priest.

'Are the others in the study?'

'No,' he said. He gave me his usual warm, tight handshake, and waved me to a chair near the fire. 'I've asked them to come tomorrow night instead. I thought you and I might benefit from a more private talk.' He gave a light laugh. 'Man to man, eh?'

He pulled another armchair nearer. The cat jumped into it.

'No, Caesar,' he said, and pushed it off with the flat of his hand. 'Would you like a sherry, Joseph?'

I was surprised: there had never been any hospitality, not even tea or coffee.

'Yes, please.'

'Sweet or dry?'

'Dry, please.'

He moved to the sideboard. The cat knocked its head against my legs and showed its fire-reflecting eyes. I rubbed between its ears, feeling the hard skull under the fur.

He gave me a schooner of dry sherry, moved the cat gently with his shoe, and sat down.

'Cheers,' he said.

'Cheers.'

'Now, don't bother us, Caesar, or I'll have to put you out,' he said. 'Put her down, Joseph.'

I tilted my legs and the cat jumped down. It lay in front of the fire and gave a paw a casual lick.

Father Louis looked through his glass at the flames. We listened to the wind in the trees, the soft roaring. There was nothing of the smart young Catholic priest about him: the holy executive. He was a shabby man, a worn man, a heavy head crowned with tight grey curls. He looked like a farmer who, late in life, had heard God in the fields. He had large blunt hands, unsuited to holding glass, and the liquid wavered as he breathed: an old man's breathing, his own soft roaring. Cat hairs shone on his trousers and waistcoat.

'Have you seen April this evening?' he said.

I liked the poetry in that: as though the season had come visiting winter, making a promise.

'Yes,' I said.

I knew he wished me to add *Father*, but I had never allowed myself to call him that.

He sighed, and took a sip of sherry. He wiped his lips with the edge of his left hand.

'You're still close?'

'Very.'

'Then that's a great pity, isn't it?' he said, and looked directly at me.

'Why?'

'You know why.'

*

The cat lay on its side and closed its eyes to the heat.

'Man to man,' I said. 'You start.'

'Unless you change your attitude, Joseph, I can see nothing but trouble if you marry her. In fact, unless we can come to some agreement tonight, I shall advise her against it.'

'Why?' The sherry was doing its work on an empty stomach. My mouth was rough, grained with the drink. The fire was too warm. I inched the chair back. 'I'm willing to have any children brought up as Catholics.'

'Then you are a hypocrite, Joseph.'

'Not tolerant?'

'A hypocrite, Joseph. No other word.' He took one more sip of the sherry, and put the glass on a table. He pushed his legs forward, and one black shoe touched the cat. It gave a soft, fire-drowsed grunt. 'Sorry, Caesar.' He put up his left hand, fingers extended. 'Shall we consider a few points?'

I finished my drink and held the empty glass.

'Be my guest.'

A blunt finger tapped his thumb.

'April is a convert . . .'

'*And they are the worst,*' I said. 'Joke.'

Irritated, he began again.

'One: April is a convert. Two: you are a non-Catholic. Three: non-Catholics who want to marry Catholics are advised to attend for instruction, to learn about the Faith.'

'This I have done.'

'This you have done.' His hand dropped. 'But in what spirit, Joseph?'

'You tell me.'

'There are supposed to be six talks, in which the Faith is explained. You have had *nine*. Tonight is the last, and I have given you the courtesy of a private discussion. Will you admit that you have put every obstacle in the way of agreement?'

'I have questioned everything,' I said. 'Is that bad?'

'It's the *way* you question,' he said. 'The hidden anger, the obvious contempt. Do you love April?'

'I don't know what that means,' I said.

'You see? Even a simple question as that.'

'I don't think it is simple. Tell me your definition of love.'

'Would you lay down your life for her?'

'No.'

Silent, he spread his hands.

'Would *you*?' I said. 'Not for her. For anything?'

'Obviously,' he said. 'Christ. God.'

'For nothing human?'

'Even for Caesar.'

'That's not likely to be tested, is it?'

'Who knows?'

I stood up.

'May I help myself to another sherry?'

He would rather I not.

'If you must,' he said.

I filled the glass and went back to my chair.

He took another tentative sip of his own.

'I must ask this,' he said: 'have you made love to her?'

*

'No,' I said.

'I knew she would not allow that,' he said.

'Then why ask?'

'I like to be . . . reassured. To find my hopes confirmed. You see, Joseph, she and I are different from you. We don't use faith for pleasure: we use it for *direction*. And out of that discipline comes . . . its own pleasure.'

'I'll become a Catholic, if you like,' I said.

He was appalled.

'Do you believe in original sin?' he said, once again lifting his hand and ticking off the questions.

'No.'

'Do you believe in God?'

'Whose God are we talking about?'

'We've been through all that,' he said. 'Do you believe in *my* God?'

'No.'

'Do you believe in heaven, purgatory and hell?'

'Symbolically?'

'Don't hedge. My version. The Church's teaching.'

'No.'

'The Holy Spirit?'

There was no point in unpicking old arguments.

'No.'

'Or prayer?'

'No.'

'Or immortality? An after-life?'

'You're running out of fingers,' I said. 'No.'

He dropped his hands.

'Yet you would agree to all those; allow your children to be exposed to such teaching, simply in order to possess . . .

'Miss April Hardy. Yes.'

'So we agree at last,' he said. 'It's lust.'

'Yes.'

*

He came back, heavily, with a full glass. Bad on his feet, he grunted as he lowered himself into the chair. The cat jumped up immediately, and this time Father Louis did not protest. His free hand ranged over the white fur as the feathery tail was wrapped around, and Caesar settled.

'Do cats have an after-life?' I said.

'I shall see Caesar in heaven. Nothing dies.' The fire and the drink had eased him somewhat, and he rested the back of his head on the chair. 'I've never met a person like you before, Joseph. You have a terrible honesty.'

'Thank you.'

'Some might call it refreshing. I find it frightening.'

'Because it's rare?' I said. 'Aren't you equally honest?'

'I do the best I can.'

'May I test you? Have you ever felt lust?'

'Priests are human.'

'Do you have carnal desires for Sister Julia?'

He laughed. And it was a free, fine laugh: the most natural thing in all these dusty weeks.

'God, *no!*' he said.

'Who, then?'

He sobered.

'That's the difference between us, Joseph: I know it for what it is – an appetite . . .'

'And you've found other food.'

'Precisely. Now, you know you have burned your boats, don't you?'

'In what way?'

'You know I can't possibly approve of you marrying April. I shall advise against it. What happens after you've exhausted your lust?'

'This is getting very Victorian, isn't it? Don't you think love can grow from lust?'

'Are you seeing April tonight?' he said.

The cat opened its eyes and looked at me.

*

Some native caution, fruit of many liaisons, brought the lie.

'No,' I said.

'Don't you normally go to her after our talks?'

'Not tonight. I have to see my parents.'

'Ah.'

'Why do you ask?'

'I shall have to talk to her. Not *against* you, of course. Fairly.'

'Of course.'

'I'm thinking of the best time . . . Get off, Caesar, please. Now, Joseph, think. For the last time. Isn't it ultimately for the best? One sees so many disasters. Think of the children.'

'All religions are labels.'

'But they *condition* a life.'

'Unfortunately.'

He was triumphant.

'There you are: you say *unfortunately*. The implied criticism. And you can live with that? Could you stand by as your children prayed to a God you disown? What about Mass? The Confessional?'

'Then you won't bless us?'

'I can't. In all honesty. I can't bless lust.'

'That's another difference between us,' I said: 'I *do*.' I got out of the chair. 'Thanks for the sherry.'

'It's not you I worry about, Joseph. I sense a shallowness in you. Survival. It's April.'

'Now you say *Treat her gently, my son*.'

He grunted to his feet.

'I can give you some more pamphlets . . .' he said.

'You must be joking. You'd have my kind in your church?'

He put a hand on my shoulder, a fatherly gesture.

'*Every sinner that repenteth . . .*'

'Goodnight,' I said.

'I pray God she is strong enough.'

'Me, too.'

*

The rushing air soon dispelled the holy smell. Out here were wind-bent trees, the starry night empty of wings and Gods, the homes of humanity where shaded lights lit hands and faces, the swishing of cars; a million people I would never know.

On the way back I bought a bottle of Beaune.

The landlady opened the door. A divorcee, she took care of herself. The figure was still there, even though the face was showing the struggle. Her lipstick smiled.

'Celebration?' she said.

'Just another evening.'

'I wish mine were that exciting . . .'

I looked at the lines in her neck.

'Who knows . . .?' I said, and ran up the stairs.

A fine smell came from the flat. In the hall she helped me off with my coat, and reclaimed her scarf.

'I said I already have some wine. And *Beaune*, too. Joe, you are extravagant.'

I put my arms around her. Warm from the kitchen, she was eatable. A worry-line marked her forehead.

'How did you get on?'

I kissed the tip of her nose.

'He'll marry us.'

She drew away, disbelief and joy fighting.

'He *will*? After all your disagreements? Who gave in? Not Father Louis?'

'He said I lusted after you.'

'Well, you do, don't you?'

'I said I loved you. *I* gave in. I said I'd become a Catholic.'

Her mouth opened. I watched the wet tongue between the small teeth.

'You did? You'd do that, for me?'

'And for our children.'

There was even the suggestion of a tear.

'Joe,' she said. 'Joe, darling, I . . . I don't know what to say.'

'I'll open the Beaune,' I said.

*

After the meal, drugged by the wine, she lay beside me on the carpet before the fire.

I began with her lips.

And then her unlined throat.

Ready from the moment I moved to the floor, I worked like the expert I was. Am.

There was a faint, final reluctance. A mouth-stopped word. And then the mask came, hooded.

I had her shirt off. I lifted her and took off her bra.

I was disappointed with her breasts. Small, unused, they had strange aureoles: a puckering of the flesh, a kind of withering. No, simply *unused*.

She lifted her head and looked at herself. Her face was beautifully moist. She seemed to discover what her breasts were truly *for*. The uplifted nipples.

She turned her quick-breathing face to me.

'Can you . . .?' she began. And did not need to finish.

I was swiftly out of my own clothes. Then undressed her.

It is an art with me. Every woman is different. Stop, have them asking for more, silently. Always something in reserve. Wanting.

I moved my lips from her navel, down.

And found her. And woke her.

She moved under my delicate finger. Lust has its finesse, Father.

She was a schoolgirl. Everything budding.

I lowered myself over her, hankering . . .

*

The phone rang in the hall.

And would not stop.

The Anniversary Dinner

The girl Rosemary, seventeen, mimed *No* to her brother as he left his position to join her. She waved him back: just in time – their father was moving through the swing-doors. She went to meet him. David, nineteen, hid behind a tower of postcards.

'Hallo, Dad,' she said. She kissed him. He had a slight stubble and he looked tired. 'Tough rehearsal?'

He switched the violin-case to his left hand.

'Had a session at the Club last night. Didn't finish till one this morning. Getting too old for that sort of thing.' He looked around the hotel foyer, the amber lights. 'Up-market, isn't it, Rose? What's it all about?'

'I'm treating you to dinner.'

'Here?'

'Yes.'

'You come into money? We'll go somewhere else . . .'

'The table's booked. I cashed some saving certificates. Don't worry – enjoy.' She led him to *Cloaks* and helped him off with his coat. The back of his shirt-collar was grubby.

'Careful with that, love,' he said to the check-girl. 'It's a Strad.'

'Yes, sir,' she said, and laid it gently on a shelf. She gave him his ticket.

'*Twelve*,' he said. 'If it divides by three, I'm in luck.'

'It does, and you are,' said Rosemary, and took his arm.

'A drink at the bar first?' he said.

She guided him towards *The Grill Room*.

'I'd rather we drank at the table.'

'It's your treat,' he said. 'Champagne, of course.'

'Of course.'

The elegant man in the dress suit held up his hand.

'I'm sorry, sir – you have to have a tie. Have you reserved . . .?'

'*I* have,' she said. 'Miss Wilcox.'

He looked at his book, the page warmed by a strip of amber neon.

'Ah, yes,' he said. 'Miss Wilcox. You'll find a number of ties in the cloakroom, sir.'

'I need to freshen up, Rose,' said Alan Wilcox. 'See you at the table.'

Seated, she looked around. The long room was busy. She was glad of that: silence would have been the end. She breathed in the smell of food and wine and luxury: this was the life. Starting tonight.

He came to the table.

'Was that the best?' she said.

He touched the tie.

'All subdued patterns,' he said. '*V-e-r-y* subdued. You look very nice, my love. How are things? When do you get the results?'

'Next Friday.'

'How d'you think you've done?'

'I don't know.'

'But you're accepted, if . . .'

'. . . if my grades are okay. Yes.'

'The first Wilcox to go to Oxford,' he said. 'I'm proud of you.'

'Congratulate me on Friday. We hope.'

A waiter came.

'Would you care to order, now, sir?'

'It's the lady's night,' said Wilcox.

'In a moment,' she said. 'Could we have some drinks? Dad?'

'A large whisky, with ice.'

'And you, Madam?'

'Coke, with ice and lemon, please.'

He went away.

'Why are you trembling, Rose?' said Wilcox.

'It's the thought of all the money I'm spending.' She shivered, then laughed. 'No, it's the excitement. I've never taken you out to dinner before . . .'

'How's your mother?'

'Fine.'

'And David?'

'Fine. Hates his job.'

'He's lucky to have one.'

'And how are you, Dad?'

He toyed with a knife.

'Fine.'

'You can't be fine in that awful flat. You look terribly thin.'

'Everyone told me I ought to lose weight. Remember?'

'But not that way: not taking care of yourself. No fixed meals. What have you had today?'

He was saved by the drinks.

'Cheers,' he said. They touched cold glasses. 'The best, Rose. Always.'

*

David Wilcox needed a beer, but could not leave his post. The whole stupid enterprise was doomed from the start. Ludicrous. He should never have agreed. When was she going to learn, to accept? For the umpteenth time he spun the tower of cards, viciously. None fell. A blur of colour.

His mother entered the foyer. He wiped his damp hands on his sleeves, and moved as the tower slowed to a halt.

She had had her hair done. It was tight to her scalp, and looked . . . unnatural. She was wearing her tan coat with the fur collar, and carried two Harrods bags. Without her glasses she was an owl in sunlight. She blinked at him.

'Why am I here, David?'

'I thought we might eat . . .'

'Eat? *Here*? You're mad. Are you ready for home? I've worn myself out. We'll get a taxi . . .'

She turned to leave.

'Mum,' he said: 'Rosemary's here.'

She turned, narrowing her eyes.

'Where? I can't . . .'

'In the restaurant. She's cashed a few saving certificates. She's treating us to dinner.'

'She's mad, too. Go and get her.'

'The table's booked. She's in there, waiting for us.'

'Then it'll have to be unbooked. She's not wasting her money here. What's the matter with the girl? Where is the restaurant?'

'Over there.'

She led the way.

133

'Yes, Madam?'

'I believe my daughter's here. Wilcox.'

He smiled.

'Ah, yes. The Wilcox family. This way, please. And congratulations.'

*

Her father, his back to the entrance, knew nothing. He continued talking, drawing lines on the cloth with his knifeblade. But she saw her mother approaching, and the breath stopped in her throat. She choked.

'All right?' said her father.

She swallowed some Coke. And forced a smile.

'Hallo, Mum,' she said.

'All complete now, yes?' said the head waiter. 'Madam's coat?'

Alan and Sylvia Wilcox looked at each other. Divorced two years, the legal complexities still a matter of pain and anger, they used their lawyers as shields, vowing never to meet.

'Madam?' said the head waiter.

'Let him take your coat, Mum', said Rosemary. 'Please.'

'We'll go, Rosemary,' said Mrs Wilcox.

'You may. I'm staying. We all are.'

Mrs Wilcox allowed the coat to slide from her shoulders. The waiter pushed home her chair. The coat and bags were taken away.

Closer to her husband now, facing him across shining silver and the single yellow rose, she saw a shabbiness, and was triumphant.

'Good evening, Alan,' she said.

'Hallo, Sylvia.'

'More drinks?' said a waiter. Mrs Wilcox ordered a martini; Alan a lager.

'What is this all about, Rosemary?' said her mother. 'We'll have our drinks and go.'

'We're here for a meal, Mum. We're here for quite a while. So get used to the idea.'

'Haven't you learned *anything*, Rose?' said her father. He finished his whisky, spun the empty glass on its base, not looking at her. 'You're a fool, you know that?'

134

'Were you in on this?' Mrs Wilcox asked her son.

'I tried to tell her otherwise, but she wouldn't have it,' said Alan.

The drinks came, and Wilcox ordered another whisky.

'Cheers,' said Rosemary.

No one responded.

'Oh, come *on*!' she said. 'Make an effort.'

They were silent.

The large golden menus arrived.

'God! look at the prices!' said Mrs Wilcox. 'Rosemary . . .'

The girl leaned forward, and Wilcox caught an intensity that disturbed him.

'Look, Mum, let's get something straight. You know what date this is . . .?'

'Jesus, no . . .' said her father.

'The date?' said Mrs Wilcox, holding her glasses away from her face. 'It's . . . oh, you can't mean that, Rosemary. Please, dear.'

'It's your twentieth wedding anniversary, right?' said the girl. 'You remembered when you woke up this morning, didn't you?'

'No, I didn't,' said her mother. 'I'm sorry. Did you, Alan?'

'No,' he said. 'See what I mean, Rose?'

'Well, I remembered, and I've arranged an anniversary dinner, and you'll stay and eat it with me. Understand? You'll *stay*.'

The intensity communicated itself to Mrs Wilcox. Her daughter's face was white bone, the eyes burning.

'All right, dear. All right. It was a . . . kind thought. Misjudged, but kind.'

'Ready to order now?' said a waiter.

*

The meal continued. On a small stage a trio played quiet, civilised music.

'Still with the LSO, Alan?' said Mrs Wilcox.

'Where else?'

'I thought you might have formed the jazz group. You always . . .'

'I need a bread and butter job,' he said. 'I have outgoings, remember?'

'Haven't we all?' she said.

'I hear you don't like your job, David,' said Wilcox.

'It's murder,' said his son. 'Manifests, Customs' Forms, ships waiting to sail, having to catch the tide. Rush, rush. Boring people to work with. Old fogeys, been there years. Covered in dust. Murder.'

'It's a start, David,' said his mother. 'Something achieved, at last.' She took the cherry from her melon and bit it in half. 'Some sort of security. Good prospects . . .'

'I'm not staying there much longer,' he said. 'I promise you that.'

'You're not going back to wandering the streets, like the rest of your cronies. You only leave if you go to something better.'

'I'll move out.'

'Move, then,' she said. She swallowed the other half of the cherry. 'Your father's gone; Rosemary's going to Oxford: I'll be on my own. It'll suit me down to the ground.'

'It won't,' said Rosemary. 'You know it won't. You can't bear to be alone. You're frightened in the house on your own.'

'I could get used to it.'

'Mum . . .'

'No,' said Mrs Wilcox. 'Don't start that.'

*

The head waiter arrived, bearing champagne in a golden bucket. The small brass trolley stopped.

'Compliments of the management. Miss Wilcox tell me it is anniversary. Twenty years. Good.' He took the glasses from the other waiter and lined them up. He turned the wire, eased the cork, and the champagne gushed. He poured. 'Here's to another twenty, yes? Congratulations.'

'Thank you very much,' said Rosemary.

'Pleasure,' he said; and left them.

'Well, drink up,' she said.

They drank. The second course arrived. There was silence as they ate.

'I found the badminton rackets and the net last week, Dad,' said the girl. 'We had some good times with those, remember?'

'Yet you still won't join a club, will you, Rosemary?' said her mother.

'Oh, I'm not talking about clubs!' said the girl. 'How insensitive can you get? I'm talking about how it was. The games in the garden, playing with Bob . . .'

'Bob is dead,' said Mrs Wilcox.

'I don't know why we didn't get another dog,' said David.

'You never cleared up after him, did you?' said his mother. 'How you tried to get out of taking him for walks . . .?'

'All right.'

'I'm just reminding you . . .'

'I don't mind playing the odd game with you sometime, Rose,' said Wilcox. 'There's a Youth Club in Blackheath. We could meet there.'

'I'm not talking about the odd game,' said Rosemary. She put down her fork. 'Look at us. What are we? We're a family, for the first time in two years. Together. Look at Dad, Mum. Look how thin he's got. He lives in that awful flat, those dark rooms. Look at his shirt.'

'Your father's not a child,' said Mrs Wilcox. 'Well, in some things he is. No man needs to let himself go. It would be a question of pride with me. Have *I* let myself go? Quite the reverse.'

'You forget how little money I'm left with,' said Wilcox.

'Well, who's fault is that?' she said. She turned the meat with her knife. 'I asked for medium. This is almost rare.' She pressed with the blade and blood ran out.

*

'Dad, if Mum agreed, would you come back and live with us?' said Rosemary. 'I don't mean going back to being married, not at first. But a family again, I've hated these last two years . . .'

'No,' said Wilcox. 'Not on your life. Anyway, your mother would never agree.'

'Mum?'

'He's right,' said Mrs Wilcox. 'I wouldn't have him in the house.' She wiped lemon sorbet from her lips. Her face was flushed with drink, and she felt totally in command. 'Look, Rosemary: it is very kind of you to give us this dinner. I know you love your father more than you love me. No, don't interrupt. I know it's been especially hard for you. For all of us. But, don't

137

you see, darling: these things happen. Two lives no longer function. They are dead, like the past, like dear old Bob. Finished. I don't want something dead in the house . . .'

'You mean you'd rather have someone half dead, like Harry Powers?'

Her mother looked at her.

'Harry . . .?'

'He hasn't contacted you lately, has he?' said Rosemary.

'What do you know about Harry Powers?' said Mrs Wilcox.

'Oh, come *on* Mum,' said David: 'even I know about him . . .'

'Do you?' said Rosemary. 'I didn't know that.'

'I'm not blind,' said her brother.

'I went to see him, Mum,' said Rosemary. 'Three, Cranford Gardens?'

Mrs Wilcox stared at her.

'I told him there was a chance of my mother and father getting together again. He said he didn't particularly go for the older woman. He preferred them young, my age. He agreed never to see you again. So he's out of the way.'

'How dare you do that?' said Mrs Wilcox. *The unanswered letters, the phone replaced immediately.*

'You shouldn't interfere, Rosemary,' said her father. 'You're living a dream, girl. Accept that things are . . .'

'I did more than interfere with Sonia, Dad,' said Rosemary.

And Wilcox *knew.* And immediately fought to deny it, put it down to a vivid imagination. But he felt sick at heart, and waited for his daughter to continue.

*

'Have you heard of Sonia Wells, Mum?' said Rosemary.

'No.'

'You have, actually,' said the girl. 'We talked about her two weeks ago.'

'My God, Rose . . .' said Wilcox.

'*Sonia Wells?*' said her mother. 'I don't remember that. I don't know the name.'

'You will, in a moment, Mum. She was Dad's equivalent to Harry Powers. But Dad has more taste than you. She was quite beautiful, if you liked red hair.'

'What have you done, Rose?' said Wilcox.

She faced him.

'Coffee now, please?' said the waiter.

'Later,' said Rosemary.

She waited until he had gone.

'I was coming to see you, Dad. Uninvited. I saw you in Kensington High Street with her. I followed you home. I wanted to wait until she came out, but she was there for the night, yes?'

'I'm a free man,' said her father. 'She was a free woman.'

'I thought: I'll never see her again. Then, one day two weeks ago, I was studying at the Victoria and Albert. When I came out I saw you standing together at the bottom of the steps. You were kissing her goodbye. I followed her home.'

Wilcox looked down at his hands. They were shaking.

'Albert Court, right, Dad? I followed her into the entrance-hall, and into the lift. Heavy on the perfume, wasn't she? We didn't speak. I followed her along the corridor, and passed her as she went into her apartment. Went back. Number twenty-one: *Sonia Wells* in that little frame. Remember, Dad?'

He nodded, not looking up.

'I rang the bell. She opened the door, her coat over her arm. She *was* too fluffy for you, Dad. Like a chick.'

Yes? she said.

I'm Rosemary Wilcox. Alan's daughter.

'She was very surprised.'

Yes?

May I come in?

'She stood aside. A nice apartment, Dad. View of Kensington Gardens. She put her coat on a chair. A little white terrier was running about.'

'Brutus,' said Wilcox.

'Right,' said Rosemary. 'A yapper. Not like Bob. It was a warm day, you remember, Dad? The place smelled a bit stuffy. She opened the glass door to the balcony.'

What can I do for you? she said.

I want you to stop seeing my father.

'She went out on to the balcony. Three floors up. There were lots of small plants on ledges.'

Why? she said.

My father and mother are getting together again.

'She laughed. She felt the earth of one of the plants and filled a watering-can from a bucket in the corner. Started to water the plants.'

Your father will never go back there, she said. *He detests your mother. You know that. Why are you* really *here? Not jealous, surely? Your father's a fine musician. Not appreciated at home: I can tell. He's very fond of you, Rosemary. Often talks of you. I'm very fond of him. Don't worry.*

'She stood on a wodden bench to water plants hanging from baskets.'

You won't stop seeing him? I said.

Of course not.

Not to save a family?

What family? she said, half turning around. *He has no family . . .*

Wilcox raised his pale face.

'And you pushed her.'

Rosemary nodded.

'I pushed her.'

*

'She banged against the side of the balcony, dropped the watering-can, and went over. I ran out, closed the door behind me, and left by the back stair. Then I walked slowly around to the front. There was a crowd around her. You remember now, Mum? It was in the paper. I pointed it out to you. *Sonia Wells.* Did she fall or was she pushed? Remember now?'

'Yes,' said Mrs Wilcox. '*You* pushed her over?'

'To save the family. Yes. So when does Dad come home?'

'Never,' she said.

'Then I leave here and give myself up to the police. Confess. Describe it all, vividly. You've both got a choice. Either the family continues, or your daughter is a murderess. Goodbye Oxford, hallo Holloway.'

The waiter came back.

'Coffee now, madam?'

'Yes, please. Coffee for everyone?'

They were silent, looking at her.

'And four brandies,' said Rosemary. 'And the bill, please.'

ENEMIES

ONE

Lieutenant Donald Russell lay on his bed, reading *Peg's Broken Dream* for the third time. He had found the book in one of the back rooms of the military-controlled brothel at Sidi Aswa, and its discovery meant more to him than the quick, professional relief the oiled girl had given him. Reading matter, for him, was prized above flesh, was like clear water: and the story of the Luton kitchenmaid who became an Edwardian music-hall star made the desert retreat, brought the sound of hansoms, the clatter of barrel-organs. God knows how the book had come to be there: you didn't question miracles.

He turned the page.

'Sir?'

He looked above the broken binding. Corporal Todworth stood in brutal sunlight, an official blue in his left hand.

'Yes, Toddy?'

'Message from Colonel Brookes, sir.'

'Bring it in.'

He read Todworth's neat, childlike printing. When he had finished, he looked at the Corporal.

'And I suppose you want to be one of them?' he said.

'God, yes sir.'

'There'll have to be a draw.'

Todworth was dismayed.

'Will there, sir? They'll need an NCO, sir.'

Russell got off the bed, leaving a damp imprint of his body on the canvas.

'Everyone will want to go. Including me,' he said. 'A draw is fair. No one can quarrel. I'll speak to the men in the mess-tent after lunch.'

'Yes, sir.'

Russell stood in the entrance to the tent and watched him go. What the Lieutenant commanded was a supply-depot, which, seemingly, Headquarters had forgotten. One day some nameless chump would come to his senses and order a return to the coast. Meanwhile, Russell's men, bored and listless, were becoming a burden. Lethargy had become indifference, and sometimes even open rebellion. Already one man had gone missing in Aswa . . .

'Corporal!' shouted the Lieutenant.

Todworth turned in the sand.

'Sir?'

'Keep it to yourself.'

'Sir.'

Russell looked at his watch. Forty minutes to lunch. He'd have a shower first. Meanwhile . . . He lay down again on his bed. Sweat dripped off his elbow.

Young Lord Fitzgibbon knocked nervously on the door of his mother's bedroom.

'Come!' she said, in a voice that chilled his heart.

*

Lunch was always early, before the sun reached its zenith. Even so, few felt like eating. The late evening meal was the men's favourite: fewer flies, sleeves rolled down as the desert-cold moved in; the serious drinking begun, whilst the more fortunate climbed aboard the truck and cheered their way to Aswa.

The Lieutenant ate with Sergeant Payne and the Corporal, at a separate table. A few feet away, another table stretched the length of the ochre tent. Beyond the tent were the mounds of netted supplies: jerricans of oil and petrol; cases of armoury; spare parts for tanks and half-tracks. And then the uncluttered desert.

Russell never appeared without his shirt. The penalty of being commissioned. Every other man was stripped to shorts and desert-boots. Now, drinking hot tea, the Lieutenant was rinsed with sweat. Once it had tasted salt on his lips. Now it was tasteless.

'Did you see the Colonel's message, Mick?' said Russell.

Sergeant Payne, the bleached hairs of his chest a contrast to the darkness of his flesh, put down his sandwich.

'If I eat another wog tomato, I'll throw up,' he said. 'Yes, I saw it, sir.'

'I thought a draw was the answer,' said the Lieutenant.

'The only answer,' said the sergeant. 'They'd create like hell if *we* chose them.'

'And our names in, as well,' said Russell.

Payne, a professional, said:

'That necessary, sir?'

'I think so. We all want to go: break the monotony. Someone in authority will have to stay behind.'

'Toddy will, won't you, Tod?' said the sergeant. 'Just to please me.'

'No, I want a break as much as anybody,' said the corporal. 'The Lieutenant is right: every name in.'

'That's *your* third stripe gone up the spout,' said Payne.

Someone laughed loudly at the other table. Holding his enamel mug in two hands, elbows propped, Russell looked down the length of the tent. It was not the war he envisaged. Neither he or any of these men had seen or taken part in a battle. The Grocers, following on. Necessary, but soul-destroying. Other men, caught in cross-fire, might envy for that moment this safety: but not for long. There was something exhilarating being close to death, or so Russell believed. Here there was another kind of death; and the laughter had a violent edge, of which he was afraid.

He saw two men getting ready to leave the tent, mess-tins in their hands. He stood up.

'I want to speak to you before you go,' he said.

Beside him, Sergeant Payne leaned back, turning his knife in his fingers. Time was when an NCO called for silence before an officer spoke. Take one brick away, the house begins to fall.

There was a silence. The men, not much more than boys themselves, saw someone equally young; but, in their eyes, expendable. The Sergeant ruled the roost. They prepared to listen, their thoughts elsewhere.

'I have a message from Colonel Brookes . . .'

'We going home, sir?' shouted one.

'When, sir?' shouted another.

Russell waved a hand and tried to laugh. He drank some tea. 'Nothing like that,' he said.

'*Boo!*' called another.

Still sitting, Payne shouted:

'Next man that speaks is on a charge!'

Total silence.

'A group of German prisoners-of-war is being moved from a holding-camp to a more secure one in the desert,' said the Lieutenant. 'They are travelling by train, tomorrow. Units are being asked to supply guards for the train.'

Payne watched a small red spider climb the leg of the table. When he looked up, he saw that every man's hand was raised.

'I thought that would be your reaction,' said Russell. He opened the flap of his shirt pocket and took out a wad of paper squares. 'I want you to come forward, write your name on one of these, and put it into this cap. Only ten other-ranks can go, and those in charge. Our names are going in as well. Later on, the names will be picked, and I will brief the men tonight. Is that fair?'

Silence.

Private Sallister stood up.

'A question, Sarge?'

Payne looked at the table-leg. The spider was motionless, as if it listened.

'Go ahead, Sal.'

'Can we see them picked now, sir? While we're all here?'

The spider moved on, making for the table-top.

'Sit down, Sal,' said Payne. 'You're on a charge.'

'No, Sergeant, I think it's a reasonable request,' said the Lieutenant. 'Yes, all right, Sallister: we'll pick them now. A good idea.'

The spider drank some spilt tea. Payne watched it, letting it live.

*

The first name out was the Lieutenant's. There was a groan.

'Any man says it's fixed is on a charge,' said Sallister.

'Next,' said Russell.

The Corporal opened it and read:

'Sergeant Payne.'

A louder groan.

'If it's fixed, I'm not part of it, that's for sure,' said Todworth.

'You won't be going though, will you, Sarge?'

Payne smiled.

'Try and stop me,' he said. 'Right, sir?'

Secretly, Russell and the men were pleased: discipline had its freedoms.

'Your first total command, Corporal,' said Russell. 'Think of the power.'

'What power?' said Todworth, unhappily. He felt inside the cap. 'Patterson . . .'

'Comes from living a clean life,' said Patterson.

'Next,' said Russell.

When twelve unfolded papers lay on the table, he took the rest from his cap and dropped them behind him, into the waste-bin.

'Sergeant Payne and I will see the ten after supper,' he said. 'Thank you.'

The men began to drift away, queueing to wash their mess-tins in the water-tank outside the tent.

Russell stood up from the slatted form, opened his shirt, and let air get to his body.

'Right, Corporal,' he said. 'Let's contact Colonel Brookes.'

*

Once the glorious sunsets had meant something: stopping the least sensitive in their tracks. But custom had made them simply painted backdrops to a long-running, now boring play.

Against that redness a figure appeared.

Russell looked up.

'Yes, Sallister?'

Sallister had the face of a girl: *Sal* not the only acknowledgement.

'See you for a moment, sir?'

Russell gave a tug at the cord, and the barrel was clean. He put the pistol on the bed.

'Come in.'

'Greene was wondering if we could swop,' said Sallister.

'Swop?'

'He wants to go tomorrow, and he'll let me take his place on the Aswa run, Friday, sir.'

'No, I don't think I can allow that, Sallister. Once it gets out, they'll all . . .'

'No, they won't, sir. They're all looking forward to it: first chance to see a real Jerry.'

'And you're not?'

'I like what's at Aswa, sir. Jerry I can see anytime – when it's all over.'

'No, I don't think it's a good idea. It's an official tour of duty. Names have been given to HQ. Yours and mine.'

'Would it be okay if I asked the Sergeant, sir?'

'Ask the Sergeant? What the hell do you mean? Who's in bloody command here? *Ask the Sergeant* . . .? Get out!'

Sallister pushed himself off the tent-pole.

'Yes, sir. Sorry, sir.'

'And what about the salute? Christ, you men are getting sloppy. You'd better watch it, Sallister. There are worst postings than supply-depots.'

'Are there, sir?' He saluted quickly. 'Sorry, sir. Thank you, sir.' And left.

Russell looked at the changing sky. *Ask the Sergeant*! How bloody low had he got? Smarten up, Russell. The only way. Everyone had had it easy for too long. Men were dying in Italy.

A smell of food came from the cook-tent. Corned-beef hash. Wog tomatoes. He smiled, and continued cleaning his pistol.

*

Three lamps burned in the mess-tent. Yellow circles on cleared tables and sand. The day and the food and the beer made the men drowsy. The sergeant woke them up.

'You with us?' he shouted from the end table. 'Pay attention to the Lieutenant. Put that fag out, Miller. You're on parade.'

The men straightened, blinked their eyes.

Russell stood up. Giant moths banged themselves against hot glass. A continuous feathery whirring.

'I had a word with Colonel Brookes this afternoon,' said the Lieutenant. 'Here's the picture. These POWs are men of the Afrika Corps: men who are not content to be prisoners.'

'Who *is*?' said a voice.

'Shut it, Miller,' said the Sergeant.

'They're men who continually try to escape,' said Russell. 'They ignore all warnings; so they have to take the consequences. A new camp has been built for them in the desert, and they're being shifted tomorrow. By train. We're helping to guard them.

'We leave here by half-tracks at 0700 hours. Breakfast at 0600. At 0630 hours each man will collect a Sten and a full magazine. The trucks with the POWs will leave their present camp at 0700 hours, and we rendezvous at the Aswa railhead at 0800. We board the train and accompany it to the end of the line. We see the Germans handed over to the camp authorities, and return to Aswa, to the half-tracks. We should be back here by 1700 hours, at the latest. A day's rations, full water-bottles, full-kit.'

There was movement among the men, a murmur.

'Are there any questions?' said Russell.

Atkinson, a tall rangy man with a shaven head, stood up.

'*Full* kit, sir?' he said. 'It'll be murder out there.'

'When did you last *see* full-kit, let alone wear it?' said the Lieutenant. 'There's a lot of slackness around: it's time we tightened up. Don't you agree, Sergeant?'

Payne, immaculate in a newly-laundered uniform, looked up at his officer.

'I think light kit would be better, sir. They're only carrying food, water-bottle and gun.'

'*And* the magazine.'

'Yes, sir. The magazine. Which will be attached to the gun.'

Someone laughed softly.

The Lieutenant coloured.

'Not until I say so,' said Russell. 'I don't want some crazy fool . . .'

'The small pack will take it,' said the Sergeant. 'We won't need the large, or the pouches.'

'I thought it was time we were tested,' said Russell. He waited. The moths whispered about the lamps. 'Very well: small-kit. But it had better be spotless. Other units will be there. And Colonel Brookes. Don't let me down.'

Silence.

'Any more questions?' said the Lieutenant.

'A railway into the desert? said Private Porter: 'how comes that, sir?'

147

'Not *into* the desert: just a little more off the beaten track.' He waited for the laugh, but it did not come. 'Something the Sappers have been working on, I believe. It doesn't reach into the Sahara.'

Sallister stood up.

'What do we do if they chance it?' he said. 'If they make a run for it. Do we shoot to kill?'

This time laughter was loud.

'Scaring me to death, you are, Sal,' said Atkinson.

'No, it's a serious question,' said the Lieutenant. 'I can't see them trying anything. They'll be watched every inch of the way. But if they do: *you do not shoot to kill.* Warning shots first; then, finally, at the legs. Right, Sergeant?'

'That's correct, sir,' said Payne. He brushed invisible dust off his trousers, and got to his feet. 'I don't think they need to know anything else, sir. They're going to be busy digging up their small-kit, aren't you, lads?'

'Right, then,' said the Lieutenant. 'Dismiss.'

TWO

The usual: a bone-cold, and mist in the hollows; a blurring of outlines, of vehicles and moving men. Lights in the ablution-tent, voices, a clank of mess-tins. Smell of coffee. A near-night fading before a pale sun.

At six-thirty they paraded, in small-kit, in a single rank. Russell inspected them, the Sergeant a pace behind.

He stopped before Atkinson, who towered over him, and pointed to a mark on the man's belt.

'What's that?'

'Grease, sir. I couldn't get it off, sir.'

The Lieutenant looked up into the thin, chilled face.

'One Aswa trip cancelled.'

'Sir.'

The rest were passable, just.

'I'm not satisfied,' he said. 'Once we get back, we return to regular inspections. You've all got too soft. Sergeant, will you see they get their Stens?'

'Sir.'

Russell went back to his tent. He took two aspirin with a glass of water, and put a fresh pack of cigarettes and his lighter in the pocket of his flak-jacket. He read a page of *Peg's Broken Dream*: Peg's success in *The Girl Who Would Not*, and the wild champagne supper that followed. Then it was time to go.

The two half-tracks were awake and roaring. Sharp blue smoke drifted. The men who were staying behind stood around, scruffy and comfortable in their fatigues.

'Remember the Alamo!' said one. 'Get one for me!'

'All ready, Sergeant Payne?'

'Yes, sir.'

'I leave you to it, Toddy,' said the Lieutenant. 'If we're not back by midnight, send the Marines.'

Corporal Todworth saluted.

'Baked camel dumplings tonight, sir. Don't miss 'em.'

Russell climbed in beside Atkinson. The hard barrel of the driver's Sten marked his side, and he shifted it.

'Let's go,' he said.

The first half-track lurched forward. A cheer came from the watchers. And then it was the dusty, uneven road to Aswa, the travelling shadows of the standing men rippling over the sand.

*

Two sights predominated: the shrouded Arabs riding camels, donkeys and loaded carts; and the wreckage of a war that had passed.

To the Lieutenant, who was a reader, both were romantic.

He did not share the contempt, born of ignorance, that his men felt for these people. He acknowledged the strangeness and the mystery of a culture different from his own. There was something about the sway of robed figures, the sound of small bells, the hidden faces of the women, the stare of dark children, the lean dogs that followed. They still held the fascination of a childhood picture: the fierce, arrogant tribesman, mounted on a white camel, at the crest of a dune, outlined against a crimson sky. He longed to know them better, to visit their tents, but the time was out of joint.

The wreckage was of abandoned tanks. Like metal sores they

crusted the desert. Where they had burned, the black heat still
showed. Rust was already at work. Guns pointed to the sky,
tracks were hanging broken arms. Men had died there, but only
the metal remained, made to last.

*

The rail-head was a single track, a concrete slab and a wooden
shack. The train was a dusty tank-engine, coupled to ten battered
cattle-trucks. The doors of the trucks were open, each framing a
portion of desert. A group of Arabs, mostly young men and
children, were seated at a distance, waiting for the play to
begin.

A number of sappers were standing around their own trans-
port; and as Russell's half-track stopped, so a green canvas truck,
bearing the flash of the military-police, came up the Aswa road.
There was no sign of the Germans.

The day was still pleasant: the sun tame as England's. Russell
got out. His men clambered down, stretched arms and legs,
waited for orders.

'At ease, until they come,' said the Lieutenant.

They unclipped their belts, rested against warm metal, and lit
their cigarettes. The sappers came over; then the military-police.
There were no officers. Sergeants talked together. Russell smoked
alone, watching the Arabs, the breeze-caught whiteness.

A staff car came out of the glare that was Aswa. It pulled close
to the slab. The driver got out and opened the rear door. Colonel
Brookes appeared. Russell went over to meet him.

The Colonel returned his salute, and accepted one of the
Lieutenant's cigarettes.

'Are you travelling with us, Colonel?'

'God no!' said Brookes. He was a fat man with a black pencil
moustache. 'Just here to see the change-over.'

'Would you care to inspect the men?'

The Colonel smiled.

'I'm past that, these days, Donald. I like a chair under me.
Office hours.'

'Any word of the depot being brought in?'

'Not a sausage,' said the Colonel. 'Our boys are doing well in
Italy.'

'What about Cairo leave?'

'Don't ask for the moon, Donald. Be happy that you're not under fire. Many a man would give his arm to have your little number.'

'Being under fire would mean I was being used.'

'Don't be heroic, Donald. Be grateful. Just think: you could spend your whole war here. Safe as houses.'

'God forbid!' said the Lieutenant. 'This is the first excitement in six months. I may even ask for a new posting. Anything would be better than . . .'

'Nothing is better than being left alone,' said the Colonel. He looked over the roof of the car. 'I think they're coming.'

*

What the Colonel had heard, and what Russell heard now, was singing.

It was a song of triumph, the voices rising over the sound of five fully-laden trucks. It was a roar of unity, and had a zest for life that shivered the Lieutenant's spine, as did, always, the sound of a military band.

The trucks turned in their own dust, near the slab, and stopped. Military police jumped down and held their guns at the ready. The Egyptian train-driver and his fireman came to the side of their cab, oilrags in their hands, and watched. Two officers came from the trucks.

'Are you ready, Colonel Brookes?' said one.

'You men,' said the Colonel, to the group near the half-tracks: 'get those cigarettes out. You four, yes you, go to the train and close the far doors. See they're properly sealed: Captain Meredith will show you how. The rest of you, load your guns, and remember the safety-catch. Come with me, Donald.'

The Germans were coming to the end of their song. When it finished, they cheered.

The other officer, a smart Lieutenant, ripe for promotion, saluted the Colonel.

'Some of them will need a leak, sir,' he said.

'Don't we all,' said the Colonel.

The Germans began to sing again.

'Noisy swine,' said the Colonel.

151

'Been like that since we left camp,' said the smart Lieutenant.

'Don't they know they're losing the war?' said Russell.

'They think it's all propaganda,' said the Lieutenant. 'They *know* they're winning – and you can't shake them. I suppose they have to think that.'

The Colonel waited until the far doors of the last cattle-truck were sealed, then spoke to the men.

'We're letting them off, one truck at a time. Those that need to relieve themselves, may do so. The others will wait, and then entrain. Fifteen men to a truck, seated, hands on heads. Is every gun loaded?'

'Yes, sir,' they chorused.

'String yourselves out, twenty yards or so apart. If anyone attempts anything, don't hesitate: bring him down. Noisy swine. Tell them what we're doing, Simon. Stress the guns.'

'They know all about the guns,' said the Lieutenant. He stood back from the side of the first truck, and shouted for silence. The song died away. In swift German, taking a pride, he explained what was about to happen. He pointed to the English soldiers, paced apart. Some of the Germans laughed. The Lieutenant looked at the Colonel. 'Right, we're ready, sir.'

'First truck, then,' said the Colonel. He threw away his cigarette. 'Pistol loaded, Donald?'

'Yes, sir.'

'Well, get it out, man. Let's play soldiers.'

*

These prisoners were the crème of the Afrika Corps. To Russell, as they followed each other off the trucks, they were magnificent. He saw them not as the enemy, but as physical specimens. They all wore the same care-free uniform: white Afrika Corps cap, white shorts, white socks, and white desert boots. They each carried a small white valise looped over one shoulder. Their skin was deeply tanned, ranging from dark brown to almost black. There was about them – and he hated to admit it – a fierce delight in being alive, a laughter and a *looseness*, that contrasted strangely with the watchful awkwardness of his own men, who were already sweating as the sun climbed higher.

The Germans relieved themselves in the sand, then joined their comrades.

'How long is the journey?' said Russell.

'About an hour and a half,' said the Colonel. He looked along the sights of his pistol and clicked his tongue. 'Never fired in anger.'

'Have they got anything to eat or drink?' said Russell.

'In their valises,' said the Lieutenant. 'Water, oranges.'

The trucks were empty: all the prisoners were on the train. Steam hissed from the engine, and the driver tried out the klaxon. The desert sent back the echo.

An MP sergeant came and saluted.

'Okay for the trucks to return, sir?'

'Wait until we're away,' said the Lieutenant.

'Sir.'

'Well,' said the Colonel, 'if you'd like to distribute your men about the train, we'll seal the trucks, and you can leave.'

'Yes, Colonel,' said Russell, and saluted. He called his men in, and as they approached, he said: 'Do what you can, Colonel – about bringing in the depot. We're doing no good out there.'

'You've got Aswa – the delights of.' He patted the Lieutenant's arm. 'All right, Donald. But don't blame me if you're out of the frying-pan . . .'

'I won't.'

Russell spoke to his men.

'Two in the first five trucks,' he said. 'Sort yourselves out. One at each end. I'll come over in a moment.'

'Big bastards, aren't they,' said Atkinson.

'None bigger than you,' said Sallister. 'I'm with you, pal.'

The sweating men moved down to the train. The Colonel watched as other sections took their places.

'There's a communication-cord, if there's any trouble, Donald. We must have a drink together, soon.'

'Yes,' said Russell. 'Well, goodbye, sir.'

The Colonel lit another cigatette.

'The eyes of England are on you,' he said. 'Ha.'

*

Russell had walked the length of the train, and now approached the engine. The driver, an elderly man with a greying moustache, smiled with golden teeth.

'We ready, sah?'

'Ready,' said the Lieutenant. The other Lieutenant joined him. 'He knows about the communication-cord? If there's trouble?'

The officer spoke to the driver in fluent Arabic. The driver replied. To Russell it meant nothing, an exclusion.

'Yes, he understands. A dead stop. But I know these boys: there's nothing to be gained running through a desert. Which truck are you in?'

'I'll take the first.'

'I'll be with my own men in the last. I'll have to seal you in: nothing but a light padlock. It'd last five minutes. But long enough . . .'

He spoke again to the driver. The driver replied. The two officers walked past the hot metal to the first truck.

'I envy you your languages,' said Russell.

'A skill like any other,' said the Lieutenant. 'Dedication.'

They came to the open door. The silver padlock shone.

'See you at the other end,' said the Lieutenant. And waited for Russell to enter.

THREE

It was already hot in the truck. The prisoners sat in three rows of five, widely spaced. They still had their hands on their heads. At the forward end, leaning against the wooden wall, was Sallister, hands tight on his Sten. Atkinson was at the rear, more relaxed, sitting on the floor, the gun across his thighs.

The door slid closed. There was a light scratching sound as the padlock was fitted. Sunlight came in lances through the narrow gaps near the roof of the truck, and through innumerable cracks. Flies sang softly, feeding on sweat.

'I'll take your place, Sallister,' said Russell. 'Go to the centre, will you?'

Sallister stepped gingerly between the rows and stood against the door.

'Okay to take off our kit, sir?' said Atkinson.

'Once we're away,' said Russell.

He rested where Sallister had rested. He realised he was still holding his pistol, as though it were an extension of himself. Somewhat self-consciously he put it in its holster.

He looked at the Germans.

They seemed trained for endurance. Perhaps it was a continuing challenge: to face each trial with no thought of failure, or surrender. Yet they had been captured ... They kept their uncomfortable position without protest, their bodies glistening.

'Does anyone speak English?' he said, and felt inferior, remembering the Lieutenant, the skill, the dedication – which he lacked.

A man in the middle row spoke.

'Yes.'

'Will you tell the others they may put their hands down?'

The German spoke, and the hands came down.

'Thank you,' said the German.

'Tell them that once the train has started, they may eat or drink or smoke, but that they must keep to their positions – not move about. There's room to lie flat, if they prefer. Sleep, if they can. But no wandering about.'

'You have some humanity, sir,' said the German. 'Thank you.'

The words were carefully selected, as though they were on file. He spoke to his countrymen, and they looked at Russell. He sensed their judgement of him as a man, and as an Englishman, and felt the weight of all history, a burden. He stood straighter, the victor. The prisoners nodded. 'They agree, sir,' said the German.

A loud whistle sounded down the track, and was answered by the klaxon. There was a hissing of steam, the men rocked as the train moved, and the wheels rumbled beneath the truck.

Sallister began to unclip his belt, holding his Sten between his knees. Atkinson put his gun to the floor and took off his kit. Some of the prisoners opened their valises, and the air became tropical with the smell of oranges.

Russell took his cigarettes and lighter from his pocket, and folded his flak jacket to the floor, next to his small pack. He drank some water from his bottle. It tasted dead. He sat down on the rough planks and stretched his legs before him. He wished now he had worn shorts. Although the train was gathering speed, the truck swaying, the air seemed motionless, as though each truck carried its own unchanging atmosphere. Atkinson, at the far end, held up his own cigarettes. Russell nodded. Sallister had already started on his food.

The Lieutenant cursed that he had not thought of bringing *Peg's Broken Dream*. Time would have passed quickly, back there in gaslit London. This was another kind of boredom: ninety minutes of hot, dead air; flies, and a continual shaking.

He closed his eyes.

*

When he opened them a second or so later, he saw a hand raised in the middle row.

'Yes?' he said.

'May I speak with you, sir?'

Russell became aware of Sallister's edginess. Food discarded, the Sten had been swiftly taken from the floor.

'Yes,' said the Lieutenant.

The man began to rise. As did Sallister.

'No, from there,' said Russell.

The man was downcast.

'I was hoping for a conversation, sir.'

Russell looked at him. He saw a man a little older than the rest. A thin, intelligent face, dark with the sun. Fair hair bleached almost white. A hard, pared-down body. Smiling. A member of the Afrika Corps. The enemy.

'No, stay there, please.'

The man nodded, and Russell felt dismissed. The German spoke to another, who looked at Russell and shook his head.

The train clattered on. Russell opened his sandwich-box. The bread tasted like sawdust, and the over-ripe tomatoes burst between his teeth. He swallowed more dead water and stood up. He looked through the nearest gap. The desert was a moving brown floor.

He sat down again and knocked a fly from his lip. He looked at the prisoner in the middle row.

'All right,' he said. 'But only you. It's okay, Sallister.'

The German smiled, came forward, and sat next to the Lieutenant.

'A little humanity and a little civilisation, sir,' he said. 'Have you a cigarette, please? They are like gold.'

Russell opened the pack, and lit the lighter.

'Think I could have one, sir?' said Sallister.

'Come on.'

Sallister ducked his head to the light, the Sten resting on the floor.

'They're to keep in their places, sir,' he said softly.

'Don't worry,' said Russell. 'Just keep an eye . . .'

The German looked at his fellow-prisoners.

'See how they envy me, sir. It is good to have an education, yes?'

'Sometimes. How did you come to learn English?'

'I like to read in the original. Dickens, Hardy. I learn Russian now. Tolstoy, Turgenev.'

'Have you ever been to England?'

'No.' He glanced quickly at Russell, and away. 'But I shall.'

'You mean – when Hitler steps ashore.'

'Yes. It is only a matter of time. This . . .' He waved a hand at the jolting cattle-truck. 'is only temporary. An unfortunate . . . setback.'

'And how will you govern us?'

'Carefully,' said the German, and laughed. 'We respect the English. May I know your name, Lieutenant?'

'Russell.'

'Mine is Fischer. A new world will come. A plan is being followed.'

Russell was silent.

'Are you a professional soldier, Lieutenant?' said Fischer.

'No.'

'What would you do in peacetime?'

'I haven't decided yet. I suppose it'll be a Labour camp.'

'We are not barbarians, Lieutenant. Your government feeds you poison.'

'Yours also,' said Russell. 'You know you are losing?'

'One is never lost until the final shot,' said Fischer. 'Are you married?'

'My wife is in Cologne, with my son.' A pause. 'Do you approve of escape, Lieutenant?'

'Not at this moment.'

'No.'

Fischer smiled.

'But in theory,' he said. 'You believe it is a prisoner's duty to escape? You would do so, in my position?'

'Yes,' said Russell. He sensed a subtle change in the words. He took his pistol from the holster. 'But, again, not at this moment.'

'You would shoot me if I tried?'

'Would you? In my position?'

'I am under orders. Yes.'

'We understand each other.' Suddenly Russell was tired of talk, of the man's proximity. 'I think you should go back, now.'

Fischer drew a last lungful from the cigarette and ground it into the floor.

'Would you care for one of my oranges, Lieutenant?'

Russell's mouth watered.

'If you have . . .'

'I will get it,' said Fischer, and balanced himself against the sway of the truck.

As he moved to his valise, the red cord threaded through the train thrummed like a bowstring, and the brakes of the engine were slammed home. Fischer fell, hands outstretched.

*

Everyone was standing. Fischer was helped up.

'Sit *down!*' shouted Russell. 'Come on, move it: sit down!'

The prisoners looked at Fischer. He was taking a splinter from his palm. He glanced up, said something; and the Germans, rocking as the train slowed, lowered themselves to the floor.

There was a sound of jetting steam, then silence.

Sallister, sick-looking, started to join Russell.

'Keep to your place, man,' said the Lieutenant.

'What do you think's happened?'

'How the hell would I know? Just keep quiet. We might hear something.'

He half expected shouts and growing small-arms fire; a slither of movement outside the truck. But there was only the choked panting of the engine.

He looked through the gap. The same deserted land.

'Should we break open the door?' said Sallister.

'Why?' said Atkinson, from the rear.

'See what's happening. Find out.'

'And let this lot charge out? Use your head, Sal. We wait — right, sir?'

'Right,' said Russell.

'For how long?' said Sallister.

*

Ten minutes passed. The flies seemed to grow in number: their faint roaring never ceased. Knocked away, they returned, relentless. The air thickened with heat and sweat. Russell's dry tongue found his drier lips.

Sallister changed the Sten to his left hand, wiped his mouth, and turned to the closed door. He put his lips to a crack and shouted.

'Hey! What's happening?'

From the second truck came an answering shout, a little muffled and unclear, but equally questioning. One of the Germans spoke, and there was general laughter.

Sallister turned his hot, damp face.

'Shut it!' he said. He looked across at Russell. 'I don't . . .'

What interrupted him was the unmistakable sound of a single shot, somewhere down the train. This thinned everyone's face. The prisoners became taut, every sense alert.

'What now?' said Atkinson.

All eyes turned to the Lieutenant. Before this day there had always been a higher authority to which to refer; or the experienced Sergeant Payne. Now he was alone, responsible for seventeen individual souls, seventeen intricate structures of bone and blood, men alive and waiting.

'Do you want to try the door?' said Atkinson.

'No,' said Russell. 'We'll give it a few more minutes. Someone will contact us . . .'

Fischer smiled.

'Ah, but *who*, Lieutenant?'

159

Russell looked at his watch. Only seven minutes had passed, but it might have been an hour.

'What about that orange, Fischer?' he said.

'That was when we were ... secure, Lieutenant,' said the German. 'I may need it.'

'I'll give you another cigarette.'

'No, thank you.'

Sallister swallowed.

'I think I'm going to be sick, sir.'

'That's all we need,' said Atkinson.

The thought turned the Lieutenant's stomach. The over-ripe tomatoes ...

'Get the door open,' he said. He levelled his pistol at the prisoners. 'Tell them: not a move, Fischer.'

Stens down on the floor near them, Atkinson and Sallister attacked the pale wood with their boots. Surprisingly strong, it creaked but would not give. Sallister put his hand to his mouth.

'Use the Sten, Atkinson,' said Russell.

Sweat dripping from his face, the man said:

'But the noise, sir. The other trucks'll think ...'

'Use it,' said the Lieutenant.

The sound was brutal in the confined space. Splinters flew. Sallister grabbed his Sten, slid the door open, and jumped to the sand.

What air entered the truck held little relief. A blast from another furnace, it soon burned. Everyone listened to Sallister's vomiting; and then it ceased. His pale face appeared at the edge of the door. He ran a hand over his eyes.

'That's better,' he said. 'Sorry, sir.'

'Atkinson,' said the Lieutenant: 'jump down and see what's happening. Find the other Lieutenant. Explain about the firing.'

'Yes, sir.'

As he left, the train-driver joined Sallister. Fearful, he looked up at Russell.

'Sah?' he said.

'I don't know. Go back to the engine.'

The driver went away. Sallister prepared to climb back.

'Stay there,' said Russell. 'Wait for Atkinson.'

He stood to the side of the door and watched the Germans. Every face was turned towards the empty desert. They seemed to be drinking in the freedom of that open space.

Fischer began to sing.

It meant nothing to Russell, but every back straightened, and every prisoner took up the song. On another occasion it would have been impressive, moving, even beautiful; but now he felt the mounting threat in words he could not understand. Soon it would overwhelm him.

'Fischer, stop it!'

But the man, and the men, continued, facing the desert. They rocked with the fire of the song. Russell moved to stand in the open space, half-blocking the light.

'Fischer!' he shouted: 'I want this *stopped*! Put your hands on your heads!'

But the song continued, exultant.

And then Russell *knew*: he knew that with the song's ending, they would be upon him. He jumped to the sand, and joined Sallister. He looked down the track. Atkinson was talking to the Lieutenant at the last truck.

'Get back!' he shouted to Sallister. 'Back!'

Sallister stood beside him. Russell could hear the man's breathing, smelled sourness.

'What . . .?' began Sallister.

The song ended, and the prisoners came, spilling out of the truck.

Russell fired into the air. Three raced towards Sallister. He cast a terrified glance at Russell, and brought up the Sten.

Blood leapt from the brown chests.

'At their *legs*!' screamed Russell.

But Sallister continued working away at the bodies, cutting a wide swathe. Blood was staining the white shorts, the boots, the desert. Men writhed in the sand. Others fell, clutching the space between themselves and the gun. The rest now stood motionless and raised their hands above the carnage.

Still the Sten fired . . .

Russell lifted his pistol and shot Sallister in the leg. The man spun around, dropped the gun, hopped, clasped where the bullet had entered; and fell. He stared up, unbelievingly; and then the pain came, and his shout was no different from the others.

*

The Lieutenant and Atkinson came hurrying along the track.

The train-driver and the fireman leaned from the cab. Steam drifted.

Men were dying in the sand.

Russell dropped his pistol.

And out of nowhere came the mindless birds of the desert, to silently wheel, and watch.